I0525452

HAM'S HEAVEN

First Warbler Press Edition 2025

Ham's Heaven © 2025 Ori Gersht

English language translation © Joanna Chen 2025

All rights reserved. No part of this book may be used or reproduced in any manner for the purpose of training artificial intelligence technologies or systems. In addition, no part of this book may be reproduced in any form or by any means, electronic or mechanical, includ-ing photocopying, recording, or by any information storage and retrieval system, without permission from the publisher, which may be requested at permissions@warblerpress.com.

ISBN 978-1-965684-52-8 (paperback)
ISBN 978-1-965684-53-5 (ebook)

Library of Congress Control Number: 2025941797

New York, NY
warblerpress.com

HAM'S HEAVEN

ORI GERSHT

TRANSLATED BY JOANNA CHEN

warbler press

CONTENTS

PART ONE

Space 1

PART TWO

Zoo 98

Author's Afterword 131
Author's Note 137
Appendix: Photographs 138
Acknowledgements 144

PART ONE

SPACE

BRADLEY ROSE LOOKS AT A PHOTOGRAPH OF A young chimpanzee in a spacesuit, lying on his back in a molded metal capsule. The ape's arms are folded, his eyes are closed. His face has the angelic expression of a sleeping baby, or a prophet at a moment of revelation. The photographer Ralph Brady gave Bradley the photograph days after it was published on the cover of *Life* magazine in 1961.

The dedication on the back, in black ink, reads: "To Bradley Rose, a moment that passed and became a memory, the beginning of a circle and also its end."

Below his signature, Ralph Brady added the name of the chimpanzee, Ham, noting that the photograph documents the moment the first ape returned from space.

Bradley looks at the photograph, gradually losing himself in Ham's broad grin.

* * *

HAM WAS PURCHASED BY THE U.S. AIR FORCE IN 1960, when he was two years old. He was raised and trained at Holloman Air Force Base in New Mexico. Bradley was his trainer. Like Ham, he arrived at Holloman by a twist of fate. While studying at the University of Oklahoma, he looked for ways to make some extra money and answered a job offer posted by Jonathan Kaine, a doctor of psychology from the Institute for Primate Studies. At the institute, they studied the behavioral communication of chimpanzees and their ability to utilize American sign language. There were twenty-three chimpanzees at the institute, and the students were asked to play with them and supervise their development.

Bradley volunteered to work with a group of four chimpanzee infants, but most of his time was spent with Elisheva, a three-year-old chimp who was being taught to communicate. Although he enjoyed his studies, attended all classes, and was an outstanding history student, he was somewhat of a loner who made few friends, and never quite fit in.

As a child, he had always felt different.

When riding in his parents' then-new Ford Eifel, which looked to Bradley like a shiny, futuristic spaceship, he would open the back window, stick his head out, then his tongue, and bare his teeth, imagining he had turned into a dog. He particularly loved being a dog in the fall—half-closing his eyes, to savor the chilly wind and the rain lashing his face. With his canine eyes, he would gaze at the surroundings and, when driving through New York, at the soaked pedestrians hurrying along the glittering sidewalks, while the changing traffic lights cast murky red, orange and green reflections on the wet asphalt.

During recess in elementary school, while his classmates played baseball or flag football on the athletic fields, Bradley would climb onto the flat asbestos roof of the workshop to read books by Jack London. He read *White Fang* so many times that he knew parts of it by heart. Immersed in the book, he drifted away from reality, creating a scaled-down, precise universe, where there was room only for himself. He felt secure in the predictable routine of daily school life, as long as he was left to his own devices. Only when something unexpected occurred did he feel stressed, disoriented, and lost.

One day, in fourth grade, his mother was late to pick him up from school. In the after-school bustle, he stood by himself until all the children had left. No one bothered to tell him why his mother was not there; he had no idea where she was. Soon a flurry of images whirled through his mind, engulfing him in disturbing thoughts that made him feel more and more agitated. He felt as though the glass aquarium that protected him had shattered, that he was running out of oxygen. He twitched like a fish out of water. When his mother finally arrived, he was inconsolable, trembling with raw, uncontainable distress. A teacher had to use some force to help his mother put him in the car, since he was shaking so much. Once home he shut himself in his room, locked the door and flung himself on the bed. For an entire evening he refused to let anyone enter the room.

In the darkness, he lay motionless, revisiting again and again how the protective wall around him had dissolved into a viscous plasma. Finally, he fell asleep, and by morning, the storm within had subsided, replaced by a fragile sense of calm. What exactly had happened to him—he did not dare say, fearful that if he spoke, if he shared his feelings, something terrible might happen, something he wouldn't be able to contain.

*   *   *

EVERYTHING CHANGED THE DAY HE MET ELISHEVA.

The moment their eyes met, Elisheva flung down the doll she had refused to share with anyone, ran toward him, jumped into his arms and gripped him in a tight embrace. He was surprised at his own reaction, since up to this point most physical contact had repelled him, but now he hugged the ape in turn without hesitation. They remained like this for a long time. She pressed her forehead to his as he inhaled the pungent odors of her small, warm body. Those few seconds were eternity to him, making him feel weightless, as if an internal barrier that had blocked him for years had suddenly lifted, filling him with warmth, and a simple, profound sense of belonging.

The touch of her fur, the steady rhythm of her breath, and the slight pressure of her fingers gripping his back made him realize the emotional wonder inherent in touch.

From that day on, he spent every available moment in Elisheva's company. He arrived at the institute early in the morning and remained there until the exact moment of closing time. The relationship that developed between them consumed his world. He was captivated by her remarkable sensitivity to his presence and even his moods, drawn by the purity of her unconditional devotion.

One day, during a lecture by a history professor on the cave paintings in Lascaux, he felt a sudden clarity. The professor explained that skeletons discovered in the ancient caves probably belonged to modern humans of Asian origin. After the last Ice Age, thirty or forty thousand years ago, the descendants of these tribes began to conquer Europe, ruthlessly wiping out the Neanderthals and taking over their hunting caves.

While their hunting methods were brutal, the cave people also revered wild animals, regarding them as equals or even superiors. The professor explained that these people probably believed that wild animals possess a primal connection to the forces of nature, a magical supremacy beyond human understanding.

The words resonated deeply with Bradley. His relationship with Elisheva stirred emotions he had never before experienced; being in her company made him feel as though he was staring into the abyss of history. They were joined, he felt, by a primordial connection.

Whenever Bradley arrived at the institute, Elisheva would hoot with delight; if he was late or absent for a few days she would express her disappointment by deliberately ignoring him when he returned. He always made sure to bring her a gift, clothes or toys, taught her to use a comb and brush her teeth. He communicated with her only through sign language. Bradley was a dedicated teacher, and the results quickly showed. Within months Elisheva began to understand the meaning of signs, grasp the causal connection between sign, intent, and outcome, and use sign language to communicate with Bradley.

While Bradley was immersed in his thesis, "The Ability of Humanoids to Express Feelings Using American Sign Language (ASL)," NASA agents approached Dr. Kaine, requesting his assistance in recruiting experts to train chimpanzees. They disclosed no further details, and Dr. Kaine refrained from probing. But he grew increasingly skeptical about the nature of the relationship between Bradley and Elisheva. He was concerned that their deepening intimacy might compromise the objectivity of the experiment. He urged Bradley to apply for the NASA project, suggesting it was time for him to forge his own path. Dr. Kaine reminded Bradley that his work with Elisheva was always meant to be temporary; ultimately, he said, she did not belong to him but to science. The thought of parting from Elisheva was distressing for Bradley. It was hard for him to envision life without her, to imagine not watching her grow up. Yet, after a few restless nights, he resolved to accept the offer.

His decision was not arbitrary, nor was it entirely rational. He was not led by careful deliberation, but by an insatiable pull toward the exhilarating potential of the unknown. It was a familiar thrill—a pulse of danger coursing through him like an electric current. His body recognized that sensation, the same one that had gripped him in the moments before he pulled the trigger while hunting with his father. A feeling that made him come alive, unbound and untethered.

Bradley packed his belongings into a sturdy leather suitcase his mother had given him when he left home. He gathered only the essentials: clothes, toiletries, a diary bound in a black cover, and a chess set he had brought with him from New York. He left behind most of the things he had accumulated during his time in the student dorms, but just before leaving he slipped into the suitcase a brown paper envelope with a few photographs of himself and Elisheva. Deep down, he knew he would never look at them again.

The next morning a Checker Marathon cab arrived to collect him. Bradley loaded his suitcase into the trunk and settled into the back seat. The cab drove him to the Max Westheimer Airport, just beyond the outskirts of the campus.

*   *   *

He arrived at Holloman—an air force base in Alamogordo, New Mexico, on a military passenger plane. For the entire flight, which lasted a couple of hours, he thought about the fateful decision he had made. While he believed that Dr. Kaine was right, he couldn't shake off the guilt of deserting Elisheva, or justify his choice.

Over a two-day period, he underwent a series of interviews in which intelligence officers and behavioral psychologists scrutinized every possible detail of his past, including his private life and his experience of working with Elisheva. They cross-examined him about the letters of recommendation written by Dr. Kaine, and pressed him with pointed questions about his political views. They were scrupulous in assessing his attitude toward the Soviet Union, inquiring whether he had ever read any Marxist books, or belonged to a communist organization.

During this time, he was also taken on guided tours to see the chimpanzees, the laboratories, the simulators, and training equipment. Immediately after the tests and interviews were over, they offered him a position as a chimpanzee trainer. They assigned him to Ham, who was then known as 65. The chimpanzees at the air force base did not have names. Each ape's identity—or, as most of the staff referred to them, each monkey—was marked by a number engraved on an elliptical bronze tag attached to a thick leather collar around its neck.

From that day on, 65 and Bradley were sentenced to live together—doomed to a shared fate. Initially, 65 was hesitant and kept his distance. Every time Bradley tried to get close, 65's hair bristled, he reared up, exposed his sharp teeth, and charged at Bradley with threatening battle cries.

Bradley would immediately retreat, hunch over in a corner of the room and curl into a submissive pose, observing the chimpanzee without making eye contact. When 65 was calm Bradley spoke to him softly, telling him stories about himself, about Elisheva, about his life and childhood. He tempted him with fruit juices, and apples that he rolled along the floor in his direction. Gradually, 65 became less agitated. At first, he allowed Bradley to approach without screeching, baring his fangs, or bristling. After a few weeks, he even began to move towards Bradley on his own, helping himself to some apples from the crate.

Then, one afternoon while he was quietly chewing apples, Bradley cautiously moved closer, and slowly extended a hand toward him. This time 65 did not retreat. On the contrary, he took a step forward, lifted his arm, and gently touched Bradley's hand with one finger. Bradley froze, and when 65's head was within reach, he lifted his hand very, very slowly brushed the back of 65's head.

Once 65 began to trust Bradley, he would come to sit on his lap, caress his face in a slow, deliberate manner, and run his fingers through his hair. Bradley's attentiveness to the chimpanzee's behavior encouraged 65 and his trust in Bradley continued to grow.

They spent nearly every day together. In the mornings, they climbed trees or played hide-and-seek. In the afternoons, they sat at the oval dining table in Bradley's kitchen, building towers from wooden cubes. They threaded beads and dismantled cardboard boxes with tongs and plastic knives. While playing, 65 insisted on certain rituals. For example, when they built towers, 65 always arranged the cubes in exactly the same order. He ensured the foundations were built from a series of eight red cubes, and only after arranging those, did he move on to the blue and then the green ones. Finally, when only the yellow cubes remained, he placed them on the pinnacle of the tower, one on top of the other, forming a tall column, until the tower swayed precariously and collapsed. Every time the tower fell, 65 would jump and screech enthusiastically. Once he calmed down, he gathered the wooden cubes and started building a new tower in exactly the same order. And if Bradley made a mistake or changed the order, 65 would get upset, throw himself to the ground, and start screeching until he choked. Sometimes he leaped at Bradley, lashing out, before destroying the tower with one decisive swipe of his hand. Bradley remained steadfast and never displayed anger. Something about 65's behavior reminded him of his own childhood. He, too, had repeated actions in a systematic, precisely ordered way. When he was little, he had always felt compelled to enter his family's apartment left foot first. To ensure this, he exited the elevator in the same way, leading with his left foot, and then advanced twelve measured paces toward their door, carefully ensuring the soles of his feet always landed in the center of each floor tile, never crossing the lines or stepping on the cracks between them.

At school, he had followed a strict routine when taking his seat. He stood behind the chair, pulled it toward him, then went around the right-hand side, stepped forward, stood rod-straight with his back to the seat of the chair, and slowly lowered himself so that both thighs made contact with the wooden surface at the same moment. If one of his legs touched the chair before the other, he started over, straightening up and repeating the sequence with deliberate precision. Even if a teacher had already called the class to order, he would not sit down until he had performed the routine flawlessly.

Every evening Bradley peeled and cut apples, bananas, and pineapples to make a fruit cocktail for 65. Into the cocktail he added gelatin, proteins, vitamins, and antibiotics. After 65 had gulped it all down, Bradley weighed him on a large scale to monitor his growth rate. Bradley had to keep him small, so his body would fit the dimensions of the pressure chamber designated for his future mission. Like the ancient Chinese practice of binding a girl's feet to conform to an ideal of beauty, at Holloman they stunted the chimpanzees' growth not with fabric or bandages but with strictly controlled nutrition and constant medication.

After dinner, Bradley bathed 65, dried his fur, and rubbed his body with lavender oil to protect it from the aridity of the desert. Before going to sleep, 65 jumped into Bradley's lap and demanded that Bradley comb his fur. Understanding that grooming was a bonding ritual among chimpanzees, Bradley's accepted these demands, and devoted himself to grooming 65 from head to toe. After putting 65 to bed in his enclosure, Bradley returned to his room, poured himself a carefully measured glass of whiskey, smoked a few cigarettes, and took out his wooden red-and-yellow chess set from a white leather box. His father had given him the set for his tenth birthday and, since then, he had taken it everywhere. Although the board was worn and the green felt underlays had peeled away from the pieces, he refused to part with it. The game focused all his mental energy into a singular absorbing pursuit, shielding his mind from intrusive thoughts that threatened to gnaw away at his brain.

During those first few weeks, guilt over abandoning Elisheva for another chimpanzee lingered in his mind, never fully letting go. The focus demanded by the game helped him to keep these feelings at bay, pushing them to the periphery of his consciousness. But Elisheva was stubborn, and always found a way to return. Her memory crept in during the quiet moments, especially when Bradley was finally in bed, after another glass of whiskey, and the chess set tucked back on the shelf. When her melancholic face became impossible to ignore, he relented, and got up again to light another cigarette. In the glow of the flame, he imagined speaking to her in sign language, asking how she was, who her adoptive family was, and where they lived. He asked if the family had children and how they were treating her.

As time went on, and his bond with 65 deepened, Elisheva's image began to fade. Her features blurred in his memory like pebbles worn smooth by a rushing stream. Gradually she lost her original form, until she finally dissolved, disappearing entirely.

On days he was not with 65, Bradley followed a rigidly scheduled, meticulous training program designed to prepare chimpanzees for space flight. As one of the ape keepers, he needed to master the operation of sophisticated laboratory equipment developed for the project: spirometers for measuring lung volume, x-ray devices to monitor skeletal development, cardiology equipment that monitored heart functions under intense stress, centrifugal simulators for ballistic flight training, and a psychomotor training system equipped with control interfaces identical to those installed in the space rocket. The chimpanzees were strapped to small aluminum chairs that faced a control panel. On the soles of their feet, they wore metal sandals connected by copper wires to an electric switch. The panel had five switches alongside two overlapping disks rotating in opposite directions at 85 revolutions per minute. At regular intervals, the disks revealed a hidden button that the chimpanzees had to press quickly each time it appeared. Above the switches, red, white, and blue lights flashed in alternating patterns, each signaling a specific response. A red light warned them not to touch anything, while white or blue lights required swift action. Correct responses were rewarded with a brief flash of light activating an electrical arm that dispensed a banana pellet from a glass tube. Incorrect responses triggered the closing of an electric circuit, delivering a sharp shock to the soles of their feet.

65 was terrified of the psychomotor chair. Each time he saw the chair and control panel, he tried to escape, forcing Bradley to restrain and, after a brief struggle—sometimes requiring the help of another technician—he managed to strap him in. These struggles were intense. Despite his young age, 65 was already very strong and when he felt threatened or enraged, would sometimes even attempt to use his sharp incisors.

The electric shocks on 65's feet scorched Bradley's heart. It pained him to see 65 suffering, but he convinced himself that the training was vital for the mission's success. Whenever 65 grimaced in pain, Bradley bit his lip and reminded himself what the veterinarians had assured him during training: the electric shocks were necessary, and the pain was not severe.

During one of the theoretical classes, Bradley had asked the instructor to attach the electrified metal sandals to the sole of one of his own feet so he could experience for himself what the chimpanzees went through. Hamilton Gravinsky, commander of the laboratory for biological experiments, categorically refused. He admonished Bradley. "Everyone here cares about the monkeys," he argued. "No one wants to cause them pain or harm them. But you must not get confused or forget why we're all here."

*   *   *

THIS WAS A PERIOD OF GROWTH, INNOVATION, AND SOCIAL change in the United States. A sophisticated highway system was being built, crisscrossing the length and breadth of the country. The voices of Elvis Presley, Chuck Berry, and Little Richard boomed from radios everywhere, in cars, diners, on porches, in bedrooms, and shopping malls. On college campuses, writers like Jack Kerouac and Allen Ginsburg drew massive crowds, inspiring students to drop out, challenge authority, and live an authentic life. Popular television programs beamed the same programs into millions of living rooms, and, in Montgomery, Rosa Park's courageous act of refusal to give up her bus seat to a white passenger, alongside many other less publicized acts of proud defiance, ignited a mass movement for the struggle against racial discrimination.

All these exhilarating and hopeful moments were overshadowed by the Cold War. In 1957, the Soviet Union launched Sputnik, the first satellite to orbit Earth, sowing anxiety across the United States. *The New York Times* likened the event to the "Pearl Harbor of science." After reading the breathless, anxious reports, many Americans felt as if Soviet eyes were watching them from space.

On the air force base the atmosphere was electric. Everywhere people talked about the atomic bomb and, when they discussed the Soviet satellite, there was a clear sense of outrage and insult. Fear gnawed away at Bradley too, burning through his imagination, tearing through his nights. One dream recurred frequently, like a refrain. In the dream, he was walking with 65 on a tightrope stretched taut above ruined cities. Each time it was a different city—once it was New York, once Washington, and another time a city Bradley did not know.

Without exception, they were all buried under parched desert sands in ochre hues. Bradley carried the ape on his back, and the two of them moved along, high up in the heavens. When he looked down at the ground, through the fluffy clouds, the scorched skeletons of buildings twinkled through golden dunes that covered the earth. He followed their transformation and noted how they changed forms, rising and falling like the body of a heavily breathing, slumbering giant. When he raised his head toward the heavens, the luminescent red-orange sunlight scorched the pupils of his eyes. Dark clouds appeared on the horizon, like troops of horses galloping away from an abyss of despair.

As time passed, 65 gave in and began to accept the reality of his situation. There was less and less need for instructive electric shocks. Bradley was convinced, or rather convinced himself during sleepless hours at night, that the ape's obedience did not stem from fear but from an innate curiosity, a trait of highly intelligent creatures. This belief, that 65 was motivated by an innate desire to learn and discover new things, deepened Bradley's affection for him.

Whenever 65 obeyed him, Bradley stroked his head and

encouraged him with gentle words. He saw 65 as a kindred spirit, and harbored a quiet belief that their bond was not merely the product of historical circumstances but a manifestation of some mysterious, subterranean force, flowing from a hidden spring that had destined them to be together. There was something agonizing about these feelings. He could not put his finger on it but, in the submissive 65, Bradley recognized something of himself. He pushed these feelings away, but every time their glances met, at a moment of respite after a training session, or before parting for the night, Bradley was overcome by a wave of heat that rose up from his belly and swept over his head.

In addition to rigorous training, the mission required advanced technological development of meticulous instruments for monitoring to understand the physiological and pathological effects of space flight, particularly during sudden loss of pressure.

With this aim, they forced 65 into a pressure chamber, strapped him tightly with strong belts, connected sensors to his body, and closed the steel door behind him. The sensors monitored the ape's heartbeats, brain responses, breathing, and skin temperature. They pumped pure oxygen into the chamber and, within an eighth of a second, the air was extracted, simulating the sensation of flying beyond the atmosphere at a height of 150,000 feet while he remained stationary. When he reached the simulated height, colored lights lit up in the chamber and 65 was required to respond to a series of instructions by pushing various buttons, this time in a state of weightlessness. Since he was unaccustomed to this disorienting condition, he failed and was subjected to a series of electric shocks to the point of almost losing consciousness. Throughout the ordeal, 65 remained motion-less, while the technicians outside the chamber monitored, measured, and gauged his heart activity.

At the last moment, just before complete darkness fell upon him, enriched oxygen was pumped into the chamber, gradually reducing pressure levels. This recovery process lasted almost three hours. Only once 65's condition had sta-bilized, was Bradley permitted to approach him.

Cradling him in his arms, Bradley carried 65 to the recov-ery room, where he devotedly cared for him over several days, while veterinarians closely monitored his health. 65 struggled to maintain balance. His reactions turned clumsy. The fluctuations in pressure caused him motor disturbances that manifested themselves in a lack of spatial orientation. Bradley spent long hours comforting him, gently stroking his back, and engaging him in simple coordination exercises, encouraging him to walk, climb a ladder, and play with the color cubes to help him regain his balance and dexterity.

He did not leave him on his own even at night, choosing to sleep on several blankets spread on the floor beside him to ensure that 65 was never without company during his recovery.

In a parallel experiment that examined the effects of radioactive gamma on functioning in space, ten rhesus monkeys were restrained in perpendicular carriers. Each carrier was fixed at a ninety degree angle, and set within egg-shaped glass capsules.

The experiment lasted thirty days. Throughout this period the monkeys ate, urinated, defecated and slept in an upright position. For the first ten days, no radiation was applied, serving as a baseline for their behavior and physical condition. Over the next ten days, the monkeys were exposed to daily doses of gamma radiation totaling fifty rem per day. By the end of this phase, the cumulative exposure reached five hundred rem—a dose lethal to both monkeys and humans. During the final ten days, the scientists meticulously monitored and compared the monkeys' functionality with their performance during the initial radiation-free phase. On completing the study, the monkeys were moved to recovery rooms for further observation. For several months, they were kept in isolation while scientists assessed the long-term effects of radiation. Most of them died within a year, and by the end of five years, none of the original subjects had survived.

* * *

ONE MORNING, LATER THAN USUAL, BRADLEY ENTERED 65's cage with a bunch of fresh bananas in his hand. The seductive aroma and vibrant color of the fruit sparked a primal craving in the chimpanzee, but his excitement was tinged with hesitation. Perhaps it was the unusual hour or the subtle tension in Bradley's voice. Whatever the reason, 65 seemed to sense that something was amiss. After all, he was sharp-witted—a quality his handlers had immediately recognized and the reason he had been chosen ahead of all the other chimpanzees at their disposal. Still, the lure of the sweet fruit proved irresistible. Overcoming his hesitation, 65 leaped forward, succumbing to the temptation.

EVEN AS AN infant chimpanzee in the dense forests of the Cameroon, his craving had led him astray. Back then he was also tempted, lured out of the rainforest with perfect bunches of bananas, and dragged off to the New Mexico desert.

On that fateful rainy night, he had followed, transfixed, a bunch of bananas tied, unbeknownst to him, to a thin rope. Like a blind creature lost in the forest, he reached for the bananas as they slid slowly along the jungle floor, until he tumbled into a pit camouflaged with branches and grass. He fell down the pit and, upon landing, struck his head against a buried rock. He lay at the bottom of the pit all night, his senses dulled. In the morning, at first light, he sat up and looked around. Tentatively he ran the palms of his hands along the wet, muddy walls of the pit. He stood up, he jumped, he tried to scale the walls. He faltered and slipped back down; there was nothing for him to cling to. After many failed attempts, he gave up, sat down in a corner of the pit, and hunched over. He cried out for help until his voice gave out, his vocal cords raw and dry. Finally, he fell silent, curled into himself, shivering against the damp earth. His head drooped onto his chest, and his eyes, once darting in search of escape, remained fixed on nothing.

He tensed up when he heard footsteps from a distance and human voices. Panic-stricken, he lifted his head. The covering of the pit was opened and through the tangled tree-tops, sharp rays of light penetrated, piercing his pupils, causing his vision to blur. His face contracted in pain. He closed his eyes and then, cautiously opened them a bit to perceive shadowy figures spreading a ghostly net above him. With a swift motion, they flung the net in his direction, ensnaring him in its tangles. He tried to extricate himself but the more he struggled, the more entangled he became.

Finally, when he realized there was no way out, he lay motionless, sprawled out on his side in a pile of mud and feces. After an interminably long time, the poachers hauled him out of the pit. They hoisted him into the air, and tied the ends of the net with a rope to two sturdy bamboo branches. Taking care to stay clear of his snarling mouth and sharp incisors, they lifted the makeshift stretcher onto their shoulders.

The men carried the subdued ape, still wrapped tightly in the net, to a small village close to the northern bank of the River Sangha, where they sold him to a French merchant, flanked by an entourage of local tribesmen. The merchant barely glanced at the animal. He bargained curtly with the leader of the gang, reducing the transaction to nothing more than routine commerce.

The merchant's men locked the frightened ape in a wooden crate that was then loaded onto the deck of a steamboat. They headed south, following the river's winding path. On reaching their destination, near a wide estuary, they dropped anchor and disembarked. They loaded the crate onto an old Renault pickup truck that was waiting by the roadside. For two days the pickup truck trundled along dark dirt roads, first in the jungle and then in the more open country, under gray and purple skies. Heavy clouds gathered above their heads. Suddenly the sound of thunder rang out, lightning struck, and then all at once a storm exploded over them. It was as if the River Sangha was pouring down from the sky. The rain fell on the convoy like a vicious predator, scattering terrified wild animals in every direction. The biblical deluge dismembered the tangled treetops, crashing down on them like a waterfall, transforming the area into a swamp.

The wheels of the pickup truck sank deep into the mud, but the men persevered. The storm subsided only when they arrived, exhausted, at the large port of Douala. It was as if the storm had never happened. The darkness dissipated and sunlight streamed down, shimmering over the docks. A group of men unloaded the crate from the roof of the pickup truck and transferred the disoriented chimpanzee infant to a vertical cage that was rusty and narrow, too low for the chimp to be able to stand upright. The mesh floor of the cage allowed bodily waste to drop down onto a metal tray. The cage was equipped with a food bowl and a water bottle holder. The men loaded it into the belly of the large ship, along with other cages containing captured hominids. For many weeks, the boat was tossed about on the high seas. The rocking of turbulent waves battered the chimpanzee's body, flinging it against the metal bars of the fetid cage. The cold, the damp, and the salt-laden air were all alien to his little body. Supplies of food and water were scarce and, in addition, he had no appetite. He lost weight rapidly and for entire days and nights he sat motionless, his eyes staring blankly ahead, silently crying.

In his desperation, he began to pull out hair from his belly and face. Bald patches exposed his tender skin and puss accumulated in the lesions that formed.

At the beginning of the voyage, some of the other adult chimpanzees, also confined in small, metal cages in the hold of the ship, tried to resist. They jumped and shrieked, they kicked, hammered, and slammed their heads against the walls of their cages. No one responded to their desperate screams. Every now and then, when the screams disturbed some sailor's sleep, a crew member would go down to the belly of the ship, curse at the apes, and dump cold water on the disruptors. Few survived. The crew removed the dead from their confinements, dragged them up to deck, and threw them overboard.

After long weeks at sea, the ship arrived at its destination and the cargo was unloaded.

The sailors pulled 65, weak and confused, out of the cage and handed him over to animal smugglers who fastened a collar around his neck and displayed him at a shady animal auction in an industrial lot located on the outskirts of Tampa, near a lake in Thonotosassa.

A trader of birds and exotic animals from Miami purchased 65 for a paltry sum and then sold him for $457 to representatives of the U.S. Air Force. From there he was taken along with forty other chimpanzee infants to the New Mexico desert, which became home.

AT THIS VERY moment, just as on the day of his capture, he was once again lured by the irresistible sweet scent of bananas. It worked like a charm, drawing him in: In two hasty steps culminating in an acrobatic vault, he leaped toward Bradley and the bunch of bananas in his hand. Throwing one arm around Bradley's shoulder, he grabbed the bunch and pulled it away. He plucked a plucked a fresh banana from the branch, peeled it and stuffed it in his mouth. His teeth sunk into the soft flesh and a burst of sweetness flooded his taste buds. He chewed with rapture, his lips curving into a smile of satisfaction, revealing a row of yellowing teeth.

Even before swallowing, he reached for another banana and devoured it in one fluid motion.

Sweetness is addictive.

Without hesitation, he waved his arm in the air, and plucked another banana. He chewed and swallowed rapidly, juggling the bunch with the dexterity of a professional, each movement precise and instinctive. He gorged on the bananas until he was full. Once satiated, he released his grip, jumped to the ground, lay on his back and rocked from side to side, lightly scratching his bald belly. Then he closed his eyes, allowing sleep to claim him. As he drifted off, he looked utterly at peace, as if the desert had been replaced by rainforest, and for a fleeting moment, his nostrils seemed to fill with the earthly scent of damp leaves and sweet mulch.

The dream, however, was rudely shattered by the sound of a shrill, ear-piercing whistle. It penetrated his eardrums and hurt his sensitive ears. Alarmed, he sprang to his feet, stood upright, and rushed to Bradley's side. Bradley stroked 65's head, looked down at him with a warm gaze, relaxed his jaw muscles, and released the whistle from between his pursed lips. The chimpanzee, encouraged by Bradley's touch, jumped into his arms and together they walked out of the door and onto the brightly lit asphalt.

As they made their way over to a black military Dodge Dart, Bradley sensed that the moment of truth had arrived. In his mind's eye he saw how 65 was about to metamorphose from an anonymous ape, a wild creature on the margins of society, into a superhero tasked with fulfilling a role. After all, his mission was designed to instill hope among the masses, to redeem a multitude of citizens frightened by the claws of the Soviet bear now circling the globe, watching their every move with the alertness of a night predator stalking its prey.

Bradley opened the car door and they squeezed into the back seat. He nodded to the driver, who started the car and then set off. Some minutes later, the car came to a halt by an airfield located at Holloman's western peak. A single-engine military plane was waiting there to take them to Cape Canaveral, the isolated NASA missile launch site on a narrow peninsula that jutted out defiantly into the Atlantic Ocean. After a two-and-a-half-hour flight, they arrived at their destination. Immediately after disembarking from the plane, they transferred to a Dodge Town Panel van that took them along gleaming black asphalt to a training compound situated behind Launch Complex 5. In the background, the murmuring of the sea could be heard, gigantic waves surging at intervals from the depth of the ocean toward the narrow beachfront.

Bradley unpacked their belongings in a temporary trailer that had been remodeled especially for them. There was a bedroom for Bradley and another room for 65 that resembled a cage. There was also a small living room that included a kitchen and TV nook. That same day they were introduced to the crew members. In the evening, Bradley locked 65 in his room and went out for a series of briefings. His commanders provided him with detailed schedules and training plans, defining goals and objectives. On returning to the trailer, he found 65 asleep in his cage. Bradley stretched out on the couch in the living room and lit a cigarette, but before he had time to take a drag, he heard a muffled groan from behind the door. He extinguished the cigarette and went back into 65's quarters where he found the chimpanzee sitting hunched on the bed, his head bowed and the palms of his hands covering his face. He seemed confused and lost. Bradley sat down beside him, curled his right arm around 65 and stroked his back with the other hand. The chimpanzee responded to Bradley's touch, uncovering his face and snuggling up in Bradley's lap. Bradley continued to stroke him until he calmed down, and even then he did not stop until 65 fell into a deep slumber.

Flight training began the next morning.

In Hangar S, a simulator was constructed for them, a precise model of the Mercury rocket in which 65 was to be launched into space. Each day, after breakfast, 65 was placed inside the mock rocket and made to lie on his back. He was strapped in and locked inside a small pressure chamber tailored to his dimensions. The chamber was then pushed into a narrow, elongated cable car that resembled a Venetian gondola in shape. After the hatch was closed, a technician pressed a button and the gondola, connected by a hydraulic arm to a large crane, would ascend seven meters into the air and begin spinning like a carousel, gradually increasing in velocity.

65 was terrified of this machine. Every time he was strapped inside the chamber his nose wrinkled, and he screeched, his eyes bulged, and Bradley feared that his eyeballs would pop out of their sockets. During these moments, 65 rocked backward and forward frenetically, as though possessed by inner demons. He fought with all his might, trying to rip free of the belts.

But with no way out, as the gondola rose into the air, 65 gradually calmed down. The intense forces exerted during the simulated flight left his mouth parched, his lips darkening to a sickly blue, while his respiratory tract was continuously obstructed.

At the end of every training session, when he was released from the safety harnesses and removed from the chamber, he was struck by severe headaches. These headaches were accompanied by a sense of imbalance, often causing him to collapse to the floor like a disoriented drunk. Nausea frequently overwhelmed him, sometimes leading to bouts of vomiting. In these moments, he would lie on his belly, feebly gesturing with his hands to be left alone. Over time, his body began to adapt to the relentless spinning and pressure changes. Gradually, the headaches and nausea subsided.

Twice a week they took him on a parabolic flight in an F-100 fighter jet to acclimate him to the sensation of weightlessness. The plane ascended sharply at a steep angle and when it reached the apex of the parabolic arc, the pilot silenced the engine, allowing the plane to freefall to the ground for fifteen seconds like a celestial rock hurtling toward the center of gravity of a dense star.

On weekends, when there were no training sessions, scientists gave a series of astronomy talks in the lecture hall. It was here that Bradley learned that the solar system had formed 4.6 billion years ago from a whirlwind of dust and gases that cooled and accumulated in the area of space in which we now live. The Sun is composed of 99.9% of that mass, and the Earth and seven other planets were formed by what little was left.

He learned that these planets were formed through collisions of cosmic dust particles that bounced and collided incessantly, dispersing and regrouping in endless random combinations that gradually amassed into clumps. Eventually some of them became dominant in the orbital path within which they moved. All this occurred at enormous speed, and so within approximately 200 million years Earth was essentially "ready," although still viscous and taut. At this point in time, around 4.4 billion years ago, a celestial body the size of Mars collided with Earth, expelling much material that consolidated and became a rock orbiting around it. This satellite is the Moon. In the lectures, scientists explained that most of the Moon's substance comes from the Earth's crust and not from its core, which is why the amount of iron within it is so small compared with the large quantity found on our planet.

After the lectures, Bradley often walked alone to the launch observation post on the eastern outskirts of the training camp, from where the Atlantic Ocean could be seen stretching out endlessly under the vast expanse of sky. This spot, where human technological achievements met the wondrous natural world, led him to ponder the meaning of the things he had just heard, the probability of the violent circumstances that led to the birth of the Moon, and the existential connection between destruction and creation. He also thought about himself and 65 in this context and the nature of close relationships—like that of the Earth and the Moon—sometimes formed coincidentally, sometimes accidentally.

It fascinated Bradley to learn that the atmosphere began forming when Earth was only about a third of its current size. Initially, the atmosphere consisted mostly of carbon dioxide, nitrogen, methane, and sulfur; oddly enough, it was from this toxic fabric that life emerged. Back then, a carbon dioxide belt protected the Earth, and since the Sun was dull and did not provide sufficient heat, the planet benefited from the greenhouse effect; without the carbon dioxide enveloping layer, it might have frozen forever. The scientist explained, in an unusually moving lecture, that carbon dioxide, perceived today as toxic gas, played an important role in the creation of the life with which we have been blessed. Over the next five hundred million years, comets and meteorites continued to bombard Earth, and it was from these violent collisions that oceans filled with water, and the organic and biological components necessary for the creation of life were formed. The amazing thing, from our perspective, the scientists concluded, is that everything aligned so perfectly for it to turn out this way.

Bradley could not help but think about the fragility of existence—that if the universe had been born differently, for example, with stronger gravitational forces, the right gases might not have accumulated, the stable elements that make up the ground we stand on might not have formed, and the sheer force of gravity might have caused the entire universe to collapse like a badly constructed tower. On the other hand, if gravity had been weaker, nothing would have coalesced, and the universe would have remained empty and boundless.

In another lecture, Bradley learned there are scientists who believe that the Big Bang was not unique and that there may have been trillions more; that the universe we live in is one of an unspecified number of universes with different properties, and that, by chance, things happened to combine in a way that allows our existence here. It could just be a matter of probability, and that life on Earth is one of those things that happens from time to time. This idea troubled him. He could not avoid thinking that randomness is what defines every event at every given moment in time.

The lectures also made him think about the strange case of 65, and the odds required for a chimpanzee born in the

Cameroon rainforests to be launched into space from a cement and steel structure in Florida. Every morning, from the eastward-facing window of his room, Bradley gazed at the Mercury rocket protruding beyond the horizon. At sunrise, the titanium rocket glistened in the glow of the rising sun. The low angle of the sun accentuated the rocket's contours in golden hues, bathing them in an angelic aura. The intense backlighting cast the front of the rocket into shadow, blurring its details and giving it an imposing, enigmatic presence. The interplay of light and shadow, thin and thick lines, hollow and solid shapes, and the contrast between transparency and opacity imbued the scene with a celestial, almost metaphysical quality.

In those moments, Bradley was overcome with awe, viewing the rocket as a sacred monument from a forgotten world. Sometimes he let his mind wander and imagined 65 as a prophet destined to rise to the heavens and return to Earth holding the particle of a clue, or a grain of hope.

*   *   *

65 WAS ABDUCTED BY DARK SHADOWS. HE STUMBLED INTO a pit ensnared in a ghostly net after a pack of wild hunting dogs had torn his mother apart. Eight dogs against one chimpanzee. They had emerged silently from the underbrush and attacked her from behind as she sat beside her cub, tenderly picking fleas from his fur.

In a horror show without an audience, 65's mother fought for her life. She didn't give up, striking out in all directions, ripping the attackers from her flesh, maiming them with her powerful daggers, but the dogs did not relent. They sank their teeth into her, piercing her throat with their sharp fangs, and left her to drown in a pool of blood. 65 heard her final gurgles as death snatched her away, swallowing her last screech. Immediately afterward, her eyes emptied of life, and her body dropped to the fertile forest floor with a dull thud.

He had cowered to the side, paralyzed with fear, but when one of the poachers reached for him, instinct took over, and he bolted. They restrained their dogs but pursued him, scouring the forest, searching under every tree, behind every bush, their voices ringing through the woods, calling for him to come out. Terrified, he fled deeper into the forest and with his last drop of strength, the baby chimpanzee crawled beneath an enormous rafflesia, a pink, rootless flower, attached to its tetrastigma host plant. Its profuse leaves draped like curtains, forming a green, shadowy cave where he collapsed trembling and remained hidden.

There was no way of gauging how long he remained beneath the rafflesia flower. Its rotting stench filled the air around him. When he opened his eyes, he couldn't remember what had brought him there. He sat up, scratched the back of his neck and felt a rumbling in his stomach. From afar, human voices drifted like a dream carried by the wind. A light rain dripped through the dense forest branches. Amid all the confusion and commotion, the sweet scent of bananas wafted toward his nose and he began walking, entranced, following its trail until he fell into the pit. A deep abyss separated him from his mother, from the rainforest, from his own kind, flinging him toward this very moment where he now appeared, cradled in Bradley's arms at the foot of the rocket, surrounded by an eager crowd of onlookers.

The hot, dry air dulled the moisture in his nostrils. His

tongue was numb and a persistent tickle irritated his throat. The static electricity in the air made the hair on his neck stand on end, giving him the appearance of a mythological creature from an ancient world.

The throng of people tightened around him, closing in from all sides. He gripped Bradley tighter, lowered his head, closed his eyes, and rested his left cheek on Bradley's shoulder.

A jarring flash of light shattered the momentary calm.

A searing white light pierced his closed eyelids.

He opened his eyes in terror and noticed a camera heading toward him like a gaping, blinding monster. Violent waves of light scorched his hollow eyes, obscuring the world's visibility. His face contorted in pain, he dug his sharp fingernails into Bradley's shoulder. A short groan of pain escaped Bradley as he tried to pry off the terrified ape.

The photographer was relentless, shooting, taking aim, shooting again, taking aim again, not taking his finger off the trigger.

65 followed the photographer with his eyes, straining to focus his gaze on the creature swiftly circling around him. The photographer adjusted his position, straightened up, crouched down, and sharpened angles as he searched for the perfect shot. The chimpanzee lost his composure and leaped in panic from Bradley's arms. Bradley tried to grab hold of him but was unable to control 65. His hair became disheveled and his glasses slipped off his hawk-like nose. The photographer drew even closer. In the heat of the moment, he went too far and pressed the camera lens against the chimpanzee's nose. The two collided like charged particles inside an accelerator tunnel.

In this instant, the light reflected from the frightened chimpanzee returned like waves rebounding from shore to sea. The fragments of information that were trapped in the light waves converged through the camera lens and were drawn into the black aperture that swallowed up everything that occurred. No details were omitted, without exception; all were collected and immortalized on the brown, metallic emulsion spread over a celluloid film, covered with sticky gelatin and coated with a thin layer of silver halide.

A terrified screech erupted from 65's throat and he lunged at the photographer in a frenzy, a savage messiah, wild and unrestrained. He bared his teeth, pounced on the photographer, tore the Rolleiflex camera from his neck, crushed the rectangular object on the floor and smashed the pair of circular lenses that had been staring at him like two menacing eyes.

The camera shattered into pieces on the ground. Glass, metal, and springs scattered through the air like fragments of a ballistic missile breaking apart during a failed test. The photographer stood aghast, but before he had time to process what had happened, he felt a large, muscular hand adhere with magnetic force to his face. He tried to pull his head back, but the hairy hand tightened its hold, leaving him no chance to escape. He crumpled to the ground, the limber, muscular ape on top of him. The photographer groaned, flailing with all his might, but to no avail.

Around them, dozens of stunned people rushed away in all directions.

Everything happened so fast. Bradley's eyes were flooded with a myriad of shadows and colors swirling and blending through his consciousness. He took a step back and stood there, motionless. He tried to reconstruct the protective glass wall he had imagined in his childhood. Then, with a savior's instinct, he pulled an electric prod from a leather holster, waved it in the air and hit the switch. Silence fell in the split second between hitting the switch and the electric charge. Bradley felt as if the world had stopped pulsating, ejecting him from this stormy reality into another dimension where all his attention focused on the flow of electrons present in his mind like thin wires spreading from a single point toward a battery connected to a red bulb, causing it to vibrate. And immediately after the light went on, he heard a scream in his head and was catapulted back into the present. With a decisive motion he brought the prod down hard on 65's neck. The electric shock instantly contracted the chimp's muscles, forcing him to release his grip on the photographer's face, throwing him backwards and slamming him to the ground with a dull thud. The ape's head hit the concrete. He lay motionless on the ground. For a moment, one might have mistaken him for dead, but within seconds he opened his eyes, groggily moved his limbs, and after a few failed attempts, managed to rise and steady himself on his feet. He seemed confused, swaying side to side, his fur bristling, directing his gaze toward the crowd. He rubbed his eyes and scanned his surroundings, until his focus settled on Bradley's figure. When he recognized him, he approached with hesitant steps, extended a trembling hand, climbed into his arms, and clung to Bradley's chest. He buried his head in the nook between Bradley's shoulder and neck. The progression of movements unfolded with a kind of natural harmony, like a child seeking solace in a lost mother's embrace. Or perhaps it was the defeated gesture of a condemned creature, succumbed to his fate, seeking salvation in the hangman's arms.

Bradley gathered 65 against his chest and held him close. He turned around and together they walked swiftly away toward the trailer, receding with each step. Behind them, the startled crowd had already shifted its focus, abandoning the chimp to cluster around and help the injured photographer. The man lay sprawled on the ground, blood seeping from a deep bite in his left shoulder and a gash on his forehead.

Their trailer was located at the southern edge of the camp. Step by step, as they approached, the voices of the crowd grew fainter, and the beating of their hearts returned to normal. 65 calmed down, the muscles in his cheeks relaxed, and his lips loosened, covering his bared teeth like a curtain falling on a stage. This was a pause after a scene of terror, a moment before the turning point in the grand historical drama, unfolding on the stage of life. The chimp was cast in the starring role, walking a tightrope stretched between two polar forces—two superpowers locked in competition, striving to liberate humanity from the bonds of gravity, venture beyond Earth's atmosphere, and conquer the uncharted expanse of outer space. Bradley felt the weight of anticipation, drawing them closer to the moment of the launch, when the rocket would break through the sound barrier with a thunderous roar, defying gravity, and piercing its way toward the stars. Bradley pulled out a bunch of bananas from the pouch strapped across his chest and offered them to 65. The chimpanzee refused, turned away, and lifted his chin toward the expanse of sky. His gaze lingered on the blue vastness distant and unyielding. The crinkly hair of his pelt was tousled by the warm breeze, brushing against Bradley's face.

With slow, measured steps they reached their destination.

Inside the trailer, they settled into a worn leather arm-chair upholstered with the hide of an old bull. 65 slipped off Bradley's lap and pushed his muzzle into the gap between the seat cushion and the armrest, sniffing the crevices of dry leather etched by sun and time. They sat and waited. Bradley glanced at his watch. The moment faded, as if the present was being buried under infinite moments that had already passed. In contrast, the chimpanzee seemed relaxed. He was content here, far away from the noise of the crowd, the blinding flashes, the pressure chambers, the spinning dizziness, and nausea. As Bradley mulled over the situation, a voice crackled over the walkie-talkie, calling them back. Bradley rose from the leather armchair, walked toward the entrance and opened the door. The chimpanzee trailed behind, his step soft and hesitant. Bradley paused momen-tarily, turned toward 65 and gripped his hand firmly. With his free hand, he felt the electric prod secured in its leather holster at his hip.

Together they advanced with quick strides toward the rocket. There was not a soul around. All was quiet. The only sound was the whisper of the dry desert wind, propelling them forward toward their fate. They came to a halt by the rocket. There they stood, gazing up at the towering edifice rising above them, pointing skyward.

*　*　*

AT THE END OF WORLD WAR II, A LIST WITH THE NAMES of leading German scientists had fallen into the hands of the U.S. Office of Strategic Services, and they dispatched a unit of intelligence agents to Europe to hunt them down. The agents scoured destroyed cities, surveyed military bases, and rummaged through rubble. They had to act quickly; the Soviets were hot on their trail. They, too, were searching for those scientists and V-2 ballistic missiles, particularly the inventor of those missiles, Wernher von Braun. They found the missiles deep in the Harz Mountains, near the town of Nordhausen. There, in the heart of the mountain, in the secret facility of Mittelbau-Dora, a production plant had been hidden. The plant had been built by prisoners of war. For many months, sixty thousand slaves were forced to dig into the side of the mountain. They toiled under harsh conditions. Heinrich Himmler put pressure on von Braun, urging him to hurry. The German army was in a tenuous position, and the realization of von Braun's vision—the production of long-range V-2 ballistic missiles—offered Hitler and the military leadership a glimmer of hope. SS officer Hans Kammler, the camp commander, subjected the prisoners to hard labor. His soldiers forced them to dig into the mountain unceasingly. They were driven down into the depths of hell, where they remained for many months without ever seeing the light of day. The incessant explosions released toxic gases, dispersed dust and shrapnel amid deafening noise. The water supply was limited, and the tunnels reeked of prisoners' excrement, spreading infectious diseases. Twenty thousand slaves died from illness, exhaustion, and starvation. Many were executed by SS soldiers from the Totenkopf battalions.

After construction was completed, work began on missile production. Three thousand ballistic missiles were manufactured in Mittelbau-Dora. Three thousand formidable black-and-white warheads were launched toward England

and Belgium. Due to their extra-atmospheric trajectory and supersonic speeds, they were undetectable in flight. Silent and stealthy, they gave no hint of their approach. Like asteroids, they fell from the skies without warning, piercing the atmosphere and slamming into residential buildings, crushing thousands of women, men, and children beneath them.

Toward the end of the war, after relentless American bombings, Mittelbau-Dora was evacuated, and the last surviving prisoners were sent via freight trains and death marches to the concentration camps of Bergen-Belsen, Sachsenhausen, and Ravensbrück. Von Braun was worried that SS commanders might destroy the V-2 plans and other important documents. He hastily buried them in an abandoned quarry at the foot of the Harz Mountains, near the town of Goslar. Shortly afterward, he was captured in Austria by American soldiers. Following a lengthy interrogation, intelligence agents managed to discover the hiding place and recover the buried documents.

In Operation Paperclip, they smuggled von Braun and over five hundred other senior German scientists to the United States under heavy guard, taking with them the ballistic development plans for the V-2 missiles retrieved from Mittelbau-Dora.

Von Braun was detained at White Sands, a classified missile range and testing area in New Mexico. Over the course of two years American officials laundered his past, whitewashed his SS uniform, and crafted a new identity for him. At the conclusion of this period, officials released a report declaring: "After a comprehensive investigation, no incriminating evidence has been found against Wernher von Braun. While he did collaborate with the Nazi regime, his actions were not driven by malicious intent but by a necessity to adapt to the circumstances, as he had no viable alternatives. Furthermore, since his arrival in the United States, his conduct has been exemplary and beyond reproach. Therefore, the military governor has determined that von Braun has been cleared of any wrongdoing, nor does he pose a threat to the security of the United States."

Following publication of the report, it was no longer necessary to conceal von Braun's identity. Operation Paperclip was completed, and, together with the entire group of German scientists, von Braun emerged from behind the scenes to take center stage.

* * *

FOR YEARS, REPEATED ATTEMPTS WERE MADE AT WHITE Sands to modify and launch into space the V-2 missiles smuggled from Germany. During this time, American and German scientists began researching the physiological effects of spaceflight on humans. To support this research, a clandestine biological laboratory was established, dedicated to breeding rhesus monkeys originally from India for experimental purposes.

In the first experiment, conducted in 1948, a small rhesus monkey, named Albert, was strapped into a seat crafted from flexible aluminum. He was wired to sensors and injected with a sedative to ease his stress of the launch. He was then placed into an airtight capsule at the tip of the missile. However, the capsule was too small to comfortably accommodate him, forcing the handlers to manipulate his head and compress him into the confined space. Tragically,

Albert suffocated inside the cockpit before takeoff, evidently not from a lack of oxygen, but from damage inflicted on his windpipe while he was forced into the capsule. Even so, his body was launched into space to test the efficacy of the parachute. Following the failure, the scientists made necessary adjustments, enlarging the cockpit, and a year later sent Albert II into space in an upgraded rocket. This time, the experiment partially succeeded. The rocket rose to an altitude of eighty-seven miles. But during reentry the parachute malfunctioned, causing the capsule to crash. Albert II perished on impact.

In 1949, an attempt was made to send Albert III into space aboard V-2 missile number thirty-two. Again, the rocket lifted off successfully, but after 10.7 seconds it crashed midair, three miles above the ground. No trace of the monkey remained. A splattering of minute particles had dispersed in all directions, igniting into flames.

Three months later, after necessary improvements had been made, von Braun's engineers were ready for another launch. On December 8, 1949, Albert IV was ejected vertically toward the stars. After crossing through the stratosphere, as planned, the cockpit detached from the rocket and rose to an altitude of seventy-one miles above the Earth's surface. To the dismay of flight engineers, the parachute failed to deploy, and the monkey plummeted from the skies like a modern Icarus, his wings clipped. Upon impact, his body was violently torn apart, his entrails and brain intertwined in a grotesque display. His remains scattered across the surface of the indifferent sea.

✳ ✳ ✳

BRADLEY LIFTS 65 AND PLACES HIM ON A STAINLESS STEEL examination table. The silver surface glistens in the desert sunlight. 65 lies obediently on his back, turning his head to one side and closing his eyes. Two people in white coats join Bradley. Upon arrival, they remove specialized leather bags from their shoulders, each designed to carry space equipment tailored to the ape's proportions. From the bags, they take out green plastic mats, spread them on the floor, before systematically arranging the equipment. They work efficiently, speaking only when necessary. Bradley takes a pair of sponge soles from one of the bags, equipped with shock absorbers made of compressed sponge coated in red polymer. He affixes the shock absorbers to 65's paw pads and secures them with soft leather straps. Embedded within the soles are thin copper wires connected to tiny electrical switches. These switches are designed to enable communication during flight. They will also enable Bradley to remind 65, should he forget, what he is supposed to do. In Bradley's view, electricity is a kind of telepathic tool, a simple yet ingenious conduit for physical communication, concealing a spiritual dimension enabling mediation from afar between one's thoughts and another's actions.

One of the men kneels down, removing an elastic pressure suit from his bag. The other one steps over to assist, and together they stand facing each other, grasping the stretchy latex sleeves and pulling them in opposite directions. The elastic rubber stretches under tension, but as soon as they release, it contracts and returns to its normal length. They repeat this action several times. Once satisfied, they move to the lower part of the spacesuit, stretching the crotch area. Finally, they sprinkle white talcum powder on the inside of the suit and approach the chimpanzee.

Bradley grasps 65's shoulders and holds him down on the table. The men in white coats stand on either side of him. They stretch and widen the neck of the suit, forcefully manipulating the chimpanzee's head through the narrow opening. 65 resists fiercely, baring his fangs and twisting his shoulders in defiance, his muscles straining as he fights their efforts. But after a few failed attempts, he gives up and acquiesces.

With the head now through, they move quickly to squeeze his arms into the sleeves, and, immediately after, they coax the latex fabric down the rest of his body. The rubber clings to his fur, encasing his chest, painfully tugging at 65's body hair with stinging pinches. 65 writhes in response and lets out a piercing screech. His face contorts in a grimace as his lips curl back in.

He spits at them.

Bradley tries to calm him, but 65 shakes his head wildly from side to side, straining to bite Bradley's hands.

After completing the space suit protocol, the men, with Bradley's help, hoist 65 into the air and place him inside a shell-shaped capsule. It resembles the burial caskets in which ancient Egyptians mummified and preserved the bodies of their kings. They secure his legs, tighten the safety harnesses around his chest and enclose the capsule in a transparent fiberglass dome. Afterward, they connect the oxygen tube, the carbon dioxide filtration system, then check the pressure regulators and ensure that the escape parachute is functioning.

Bradley observes them, making sure that 65 remains obedient. The sight of the restrained chimp fills him with pity, reminding him of a painting he saw in an art book, or perhaps a slide in a university lecture on the Baroque period. In this particular painting, which he now cannot get out of his head, a helpless white lamb lies on a stone bench against a completely black background, its legs bound with rope, its head resting submissively on the hard surface.

As the preparation protocol comes to an end, the men in white coats lift the capsule and carry 65 toward the elevator that will take him up to the top of the launch tower. Bradley steps closer, smiles, and offers a look of farewell. Their eyes lock. Bradley is cherishing the moment, trying to eternalize it in his mind.

Bradley thrusts his hand into his pants pocket and touches a tangled shoelace. He rubs one finger along the lace's ridges, feels the fabric's texture, and, without thinking, wraps it around his ring finger. The lace tightens around his finger like a snake, constricting with each pass and cutting off the blood supply. Undeterred, he continues to tighten the lace until the blood flow to his finger is almost cut off, all the time, using his thumb to feel the trapped fingertip harden. The finger grows cold as the pain intensifies, but he doesn't relent.

He slowly removes his hand from the pocket, carefully examines the pale finger, then abruptly in a sudden motion releases his grip. The lace slackens instantly, like a coil unraveling, and blood rushes back with a surge of warmth. Red blood cells rich with oxygen flood the numbed finger, bringing it back to life with a sharp sensation of pins and needles.

The elevator door opens. The men in white carry 65 to a narrow shaft. They press a button and the door closes, swallowing them up behind an iron screen. Bradley remains alone, watching the elevator as it ascends toward the top of the missile, following the steel cables coiling around a large wheel powered by an electric motor.

He tries to calm his nerves, to eliminate dark thoughts from his mind, prophecies that might become self-fulfilling.

He longs for everything to end well. He reminds himself of the successful flights of Miss Able and Miss Baker—two small monkeys launched two years earlier aboard a Jupiter missile, essentially an upgraded V-2, to examine the effects of cosmic radiation on living creatures in space. Both monkeys returned safely, and presumably, Miss Able would still be alive today had her heart not stopped due to an anesthetic injected into her vein during a procedure to remove electrodes that had been implanted for monitoring purposes.

Miss Baker, on the other hand, survived, and now lives among a family of squirrel monkeys in the laboratory's zoo. As Bradley ponders the journey of Miss Able and Miss Baker, the elevator comes to a gentle halt. The door opens and he watches from a distance as the two men in white guide the capsule to the cockpit at the tip of the missile. After positioning 65, they scan the control panels, check the electrodes and sensors, and examine the indicator lights, levers, and switches.

Bradley doesn't take his eyes off them, watching from a distance as the elevator door closes. He tracks the elevator's descent to the ground, the men in white returning home after completing their task.

On his way to the control room, Bradley stops beside a Brazilian peppertree growing at the side of the path. He turns his head and, with a fleeting glance, surveys the area.

After ensuring no one else is around, he unzips his military pants and urinates on the invasive shrub. The simple act brings a sense of relief, releasing some of the tension he's been carrying. He listens to the trickle, following the golden droplets of urine as they bounce and drip on the pepper-tree's green leaves, fall onto the ground, and are absorbed into the soil.

The control room is densely packed with mathematicians, physicists, engineers, designers, radio technicians, radio monitors, telephonists, control officers, technical signalers, veterinarians. All are alert, their eyes fixed on the screens, on the control panels. Everyone is closely monitoring 65's physiological state, his breathing, body temperature, blood pressure, and heart rate.

Bradley trains his eyes on the flickering lines of the control panels, asymmetric graphics of electrical frequencies. A computerized visualization of electromagnetic fields, waves flowing monotonically across screens in a universe without beginning or end, a world in which time seems suspended.

Suddenly the assertive voice of flight director Chris Sharp interrupts the silence, and immediately afterward the countdown begins. Ten, nine, eight, seven…

Six, five.

Bradley absorbs the descending numbers. It is as though time is changing direction, running in reverse like a movie screened backward, and all the images compress and pile one on top of the other, crushing each other, collapsing and crashing like a tower unable to withstand the load.

Four…

He closes his eyes, terrified of the impending calamity. In the background, the incessant ticking of clocks.

Three…

And then, all at once, it is over. The countdown comes to a halt in a deafening silence that sucks the air from his lungs. He opens his eyes and stares into the vacuum that has formed.

He looks around.

For a split second, it seems to Bradley that those present have frozen in place. This illusion is shattered by the thunderous voice of a flight controller announcing over the loudspeaker that the aerospace engineers have located a malfunction in the reverse current protection device, and that the launch will be delayed.

Bradley takes his eyes off the flight controller and scans the room. He observes the event from the side, following the veterinarians, noting them watching the chimpanzee through the screens, recording 65's vital signs, and reporting that he appears calm. His condition is stable.

Bradley feels stifled. Cold sweat forms on his brow. He gets up and leaves the room.

It is past midnight, and dark outside. Bands of stars glitter, celestial strands of light. He walks toward a lone palm tree standing tall in the building's parking lot, removes a cigarette from a red Winston pack in his shirt pocket, places the filter between his lips, and lights up.

He raises his head, exhales a stream of smoke from his lungs and gazes at the stars through the thick, curling screen of smoke.

His face is illuminated by the flare of the match. He lowers his head, exhales again, extinguishes the flame, and is engulfed in darkness. When he raises his head again and scans the sky, he immediately locates the Big Dipper, and like an echo chamber, it takes him back to a distant summer day when he was eleven years old.

1940, NEW YORK.

It was the first summer holiday since his father had packed a suitcase and left home.

He had left just days after Christmas. His mother did not speak about it, and he learned quickly, from her persistent silence, not to ask. At first she became very quiet, tending only to what was necessary. Her voice was measured, her gestures careful, as if any excess warmth might undo something she was trying to hold together.

For a few weeks, they existed side by side, speaking only when needed. As if she had demanded, without words, to keep a certain distance.

Then, as spring turned, something shifted.

No explanations, no acknowledgments. Just a slow return to something almost familiar.

On that summer morning, when he entered the kitchen, she put a plate of pancakes in front of him and told him that she had a surprise.

That afternoon, they walked together toward Madison Square Garden, on the west side of 8th Avenue, between 49th and 50th Streets. They were going to see a famous circus, the Ringling Bros. and Barnum & Bailey. He caught his breath as they entered the gates. The air was thick with scents, a blend of sawdust, sweet cotton candy, and animal dung. His heart beat wildly when the spotlights came on, flooding the ring with blinding light. From out of the shadows stepped a mustachioed ringmaster, dressed in a long tailcoat and black top hat. With the agility of a leprechaun, he leaped to the center of the stage and welcomed the audience. In a rollicking voice he proudly announced that, in just a moment, the greatest and most spectacular show on earth would be revealed.

The opening parade began as he spoke. A procession of horses burst in and galloped around the ring. Following the horses was a troupe of clowns on stilts, their long legs in colorful pants tottering precariously in the air, and behind them, mustachioed giants hoisted dwarfs onto their shoulders. Next to the giants walked graceful women in tight-fitting, sparkling bodysuits that accentuated their curves, followed by a herd of elephants adorned with glittering saddles. Above the parade stretched a tangle of wires and trapezes, like the latticed infrastructure of elevated railroad tracks.

Right after the ceremony ended, the ring emptied, and after a short interlude, the ringmaster returned, removed the top hat from his head, and beckoned with his hand to a troupe of brown bears.

Bradley was amazed to see bears gliding on roller skates to the center of the arena, dressed in short tutus, frolicking like children in a playground. When multicolored beach balls were thrown into the ring, the bears jumped on the balls and glided across the stage, balancing with the ease of dragonflies hovering over puddles of water. The audience went wild, cheering with tumultuous applause even after the bears took a bow and left the ring.

As the act ended, the lights dimmed, and through the darkness a narrow beam of light was cast, a golden shaft, illuminating the ringmaster. He stood at the center of the stage, motionless. Only after the drumroll ended did he open his mouth and declare in a tense, electrified voice that, in a few short moments, the world's most terrifying living creature would enter the stage. As soon as he finished speaking, the lights came on, the red velvet curtains were drawn back, and to the steady rhythm of a military march, a pair of clowns entered the ring, followed by a procession of six white horses pulling a carriage upon which a large box had been placed, covered in a cloth decorated with a picture depicting a lavish banquet in a forest set in an opulent landscape. The ringmaster went up to the carriage and removed the painted cloth with a flourish, revealing a huge glass tank underneath it.

And then, in a spectacle worthy of a magic show, a giant gorilla with a silvery back and a scarred face was revealed to the audience. Written in large, gilded Gothic letters at the lower edge of the tank was *Gargantua the Great Gorilla*. The exposed ape seemed lost, restlessly circling the walls of the transparent container. Silence fell, and when the procession passed right in front of Bradley and his mother, the gorilla's eyes met Bradley's. Gargantua froze and shot Bradley a piercing look. Bradley did not avert his gaze; he stared right into the depths of the gorilla's eyes, which seemed to him like a bottomless abyss of the creature's dark loneliness.

That night, he dreamed that the glass walls of the container were closing in on the gorilla, and he watched the gorilla hurling himself at the walls, trying to break free. Finally, with no way out, the gorilla despaired and gave up. The next day, he read in the circus program his mother had bought him that Gargantua the Great Gorilla had been captured in the Belgian Congo. Missionaries, who had bought the gorilla from poachers, had given him to a captain named Arthur Phillips. The skipper grew fond of the gorilla, and he became popular among most of the crew. But one evening, a drunken sailor, annoyed that the gorilla was ignoring him, picked up from the engine room a small container of nitric acid and threw the liquid in the gorilla's face. The acid burned the ape's flesh and left scars that distorted his face and gave him a frightening look. Once the ship arrived in America, word of the monstrous gorilla reached the ears of John Ringling, a shrewd circus owner. Sensing an opportunity in the animal's haunting appearance, he bought the gorilla from the sailors, who had no further use for it. He named him Gargantua, after the entertaining giant from the books of François Rabelais. Unlike the gorilla, however, Rabelais' protagonist was a hedonistic creature, a rebel and a freedom fighter. Ringling plastered the gorilla's face all over town. He spread exaggerated stories about him that contained not a shred of truth, depicting him as a terrifying, dangerous, and violent creature. As a marketing stunt, Ringling made an astute decision; massive crowds rushed in to see the raging giant. This surge in attendance spared the circus from bankruptcy during the Great Depression.

KRAFT'S VOICE IS announcing over the intercom that the malfunction has been fixed. He raises his head, glances briefly at the Big Dipper suspended in the night sky, and hurries back to the control center. He enters the room and navigates his way between the laden tables. Three hours have passed since he left the room, but it seems to Bradley that nothing has changed. Flight engineers report that the problem has been checked and corrected. Chris Sharp asks for patience, and announces that a decision has been made to further delay the launch, until sunrise. He orders crew members to take their positions and remain alert.

The room is quiet. The rocket too.

65, however, is not. He shifts agitatedly from side to side; Bradley tries to calm him by talking in a comforting voice through the microphone. The ape listens, falls silent, calms down, and then becomes distressed again. Two hours later, the green light comes on in the control room. Chris Sharp orders everyone to prepare and declares a five-minute countdown to launch. The crew members perform final checks. Two minutes later, the fuel and the liquid oxygen valves open. The flight controller confirms that the ethanol gas has ignited, and immediately after that, the external power supplies disconnect, and the internal batteries kick in. The rocket's engines ignite with a deafening noise. 65 is startled and jerks forward, but the tight safety belts hold him back. His face contorts, his nose wrinkles, and a moan of pain escapes his wide, open mouth, swallowed by the thunderous roar of the jet engines.

Liquid fuel is compressed into the combustion chambers from a large tank. Ethanol gas sprays out in a jet thrust through the neck of a narrow nozzle and ascends, as compressed liquid oxygen flows along from a second tank. The gases rush forward toward each other, flowing through a closed system toward a final, inevitable, and fateful encounter destined to occur inside the combustion chamber. There, they will explode in a wild frenzy, burning to the sound of trembling thunder.

The blaze of the burners pushes down, ripping the rocket away from the ground. Opposing gravitational forces struggle to hold on to the rocket but inevitably Earth surrenders to the sheer escape force and the rocket shoots upwards at a right angle. It is engulfed by billows of dense smoke and eventually fades from view.

Bradley and the crew members follow the rocket intently as it hurtles into the sky at a speed of five thousand miles per hour. Gravitational forces compress 65, generating extreme pressure on his bones, flattening his face, and sucking the air from his lungs. He struggles to breathe, struggles to move his limbs. Bradley's eyes are riveted to the screen, tracking the fiery rocket as it recedes. Within a few seconds, the rocket becomes a faint speck in space and then disappears into the abyss of the sky.

The space engineers announce that a problem has been detected in the fuel injection pump. Jason Pate, chief engineer, reports that the malfunction is causing flammable liquid to be compressed into the combustion chamber with excessive force. The flames in the compressors intensify, raising the temperature and causing hot gases to be ejected under pressure through the injection nozzle. The problem has triggered an acceleration in the rocket's speed and a change to its angle of ascent. The sudden acceleration instantly increases the pressure of gravitational forces; within seconds, it surges to 17G, seventeen times the weight of the chimpanzee's body, crushing his head, squeezing his heart, and increasing his pulse rate. This causes atrial fibrillation as blood is forced downward, draining into his legs. Bradley covers his face with his hands. He feels as though *his* eyes, not 65's, are being pressed into their sockets. Meanwhile, 65's peripheral facial muscles twitch wildly, his cheeks tremble. On the monitors, he looks like a psychotic passenger on a devil's train hurtling toward hell. Another minute passes. 65 becomes apathetic. Chris Sharp fears losing him. But then, with mechanical precision, the emergency battery kicks in, closing an electrical circuit and sending a current of electrons through the wires woven into the soles of the chimpanzee's feet. He is dazed but when the electric shock contracts his heart muscle, he begins to respond again. A few more seconds pass. The rocket exits the exosphere and, in an instant, everything turns upside down. Gravity dissipates, and 65 is sucked into the void. He experiences immediate relief because now, detached from the burden of his body, he floats like a feather in space, his limbs relaxing and his fur billowing. Warm blood flows back into his arteries. His eyes open and his vision clears. Within the cosmic, spatial silence, sensations of space and time dissolve. Above him, unfathomable darkness; below, a wondrous display of sunsets melting into burning sunrises. His mind foggy, he teeters between consciousness and reverie. His face swells, his vision blurs. Tears flow from his eyes, streaming along the arc of his cornea. They do not trickle down; instead, they accumulate in the shadow of the bridge of his nose. He sinks down into the darkness, plunging through large rainforest trees, some upright, some bent, but all, without exception, towering over the dense undergrowth of the jungle. His nostrils fill with the forgotten perfumes of large flowers, slivers of wet bark on tree trunks, damp moss, morning dew. He hears birds chirping, and wind rustling through the ferns. He blinks, his eyelids gliding over his eyeballs, banishing the veil of tears. His vision returns, and he feels the blood in his body flowing from capillaries to veins, up the canals, as if embarking on a journey from the soles of his feet to his head.

In the control room, they announce that the ape has

stabilized and is now in zero gravity. In other words, he is in
free fall. Bradley is concerned, clenching his fist, his thumb
stretched out as if he is about to hit the activation switch.
The emergency system responds with precision, releasing
an electric current that sears through 65's body, jolting him
back to consciousness. He immediately responds to the
flashing lights, deftly pressing the illuminated buttons and
pulling the levers, as Bradley had taught him back at the
training base. Now, however, he is alone in the universe.

When Hamilton Garbinsky, head of the Biological
Research Unit, first came up with the idea of sending a
chimpanzee into space, everyone mocked him, thinking he
had lost his mind. Despite this, Garbinsky pressed on, never
giving up. With single-minded determination he ordered
his subordinates to proceed. They had no choice but to
put their faith in him. And now, against all odds, they are
witnessing the realization of his vision, in which the chosen
chimpanzee proves to them, on behalf of all hominids, the
superiority of his species.

65 and Bradley are now working in tandem, transformed
into one, like a pair of stuntmen walking toward each other
on a tightrope stretched above a chasm. Together, they
pass by and sink down, sink down and pass by. 65 has been
flying in space for six minutes now, moving rapidly above
the curved, receding horizon of Earth. Floating weightlessly
among the ultraviolet rays that absorb and destroy the
myriad colors of the rainbow, enshrouding his capsule in a
hazy mist.

The chimpanzee tremors and shakes, and immediately
afterward atmospheric braking begins, accompanied by
waves of heat. The sudden braking causes the spacecraft's

nose to spin, and as a result, it decreases its rate of descent. The atmospheric friction generated causes the heat shields to glow; fiberglass, aluminum, and beryllium chips scatter everywhere. 65's heart is now beating hard; blood flows from it, washing through his body like a waterfall cascading from his head to his legs. His vision blurs again in the searing sunlight. Light waves of white light penetrate his retinas, diffusing within them innumerable glowing photons, each with its own identity and trajectory.

A deep, almost palpable silence fills the control room. Hundreds of people on the ground are following what is happening with bated breath, watching the screens, waiting for a sign, like a philharmonic orchestra waiting for the conductor's cue. When the capsule has descended to an altitude of 21,000 feet, a small parachute opens and everyone holds their breath. At an altitude of 10,000 feet, to sighs of relief and enthusiastic applause, the main parachute also opens with a sudden jerk that jolts 65's spinal column. His vertebrae vibrate around shuddering cartilage. All at once, his fall slows down and the pressure exerted on his body rescinds.

His eyes widen, flooded with light waves in hues of blue sky and water. From the ground, the control team watches the ape that fell from space, trapped like a bird inside a steel cage, under the shade of the parachute's canopy.

And then, just a moment before the capsule touches down in the water, an airbag inflates under the heat shield, and simultaneously, the parachute detaches, and a fluorescent green pigment is released from a container connected to the bottom of the module, dyeing the turbulent foam that spreads across the waves. The phosphorescent color dissolves in the water and stains the azure sea with an acidic hue. A spotlight switches on, flashing atop the capsule, additional balloons inflate around the nozzle, and immediately after, with a violent bang, the cockpit lands on the surface of the water. The impact pushes the water away; a returning wave washes over the capsule with white foam. The force of the landing tears the shock absorbers from the cockpit's body. Minuscule cracks form along the titanium walls, allowing seawater to seep inside, pooling in the belly of the vessel.

The murmur of rushing water stimulates 65's parched lips. He has not had a drink for hours. He reaches out as far as he can go. His tongue is dry, sticking to his palate, but he doesn't give up, and with a supreme effort, he achieves his goal and immerses the tip of his thumb in the wet puddle. The touch of cold water energizes his body. In a swift motion, he raises his hand and sticks the wet finger between his scorched lips. The salt stings the exposed skin, his nose wrinkles, and the wail of a desperate prisoner escapes his throat. Larger waves hit the sides of the capsule, causing it ultimately to flip onto its side. The loose heat shield that swayed creakily above his head is torn from the ceiling, crashes onto his face, cutting a deep gash on the bridge of his nose.

Blood flows from the wound, dripping into the rising pool of seawater at the bottom of the box. The blood spreads across his face, trickling down the eye sockets. He closes his eyes and rubs them, but the blood coagulates and glues the eyelids closed.

Bradley gets up from his seat and walks over to the radar technician. The technician notices him and looks up. Bradley seizes the opportunity and, quickly, asks after 65.

"We've lost him," the technician replies. His answer sounds like a dark riddle. Bradley falters and then asks,

"What do you mean, we've lost him?"

The technician is silent for a moment. "Currently, we're not detecting him on the radar," he finally says. He turns his back to Bradley to track the flickering electronic signals on the screen.

Chris Sharp orders Bradley to return to his seat. Bradley watches him as he consults with a team of engineers, takes a walkie-talkie and contacts the captain of the Donner rescue ship, requesting assistance. From the Donner, two helicopters are launched into the air, all visible on one of the screens in the control room. The choppers circle, apparently scanning the surface of the sea.

The spacecraft continues to sink; soon it will be swallowed by the sea. And the chimp, after soaring to such heights, sinks with it.

One of the chopper pilots detects a flashing light in the distance and reports it over the walkie-talkie. He locates the spacecraft at a distance of thirty-seven miles northeast of the rescue ship. As the ground crew watches on their screens, he approaches the spacecraft, descends, and then hovers above it. Waves rising to a height of five feet slam against the sides of the capsule, causing it to sway from side to side.

Wind from the helicopter's rotor blades slowly sets the capsule spinning around. Searchlight beams penetrate through a slot, dancing erratically on an inner wall. The helicopter door opens, and a diver is lowered via a rope toward the water below. The waves threaten to slam the diver against the steel wall, covering the capsule in gray and white foam. With hands and feet he tries to stay away from the capsule and steady himself. Finally, in a great effort, he grabs hold of the titanium loops welded above the doorway.

He clings to the side of the spacecraft, connects the hook of a thick steel cable to one of the loops, and signals to the pilot with one hand. After the diver is pulled back up from the water, the helicopter rises into the air. The capsule and the chimpanzee inside are lifted up, swaying from side to side like the pendulum of a clock, dividing the continuous flow of time into a steady rhythm of measured segments. Water gushes through the gashes into the capsule's hull. Sea water spills back into the ocean.

Bradley leaves the control room, walks to the landing pad, climbs into a waiting chopper, and buckles his seat belt. The pilot revs up the engines. The rotor spins on its axis faster and faster, the blades slicing through the air as the helicopter rises above the ground. Their chopper is the first to land on the rescue ship. Bradley waits for the pilot's permission, unbuckles his seat belt, opens the door, and descends onto the smooth steel deck of the ship, ducking his head to keep it away from the roaring blades spinning above him. In the distance, he sees the approaching chopper with the capsule suspended from it, swinging through the air and twirling around.

The rescue helicopter now circles above their heads. The ground crew clears the landing pad and instructs bystanders to move away. A cloud of dust rises into the air, merging with drops of water and salt. The capsule casts a shadow on the deck, the chopper descends with ear-splitting thunder, and after a series of delicate maneuvers, deposits the capsule on the stern of the deck. The ground crew disconnects the cables, and the pilot sets down the chopper near the capsule. The rescue team now works quickly. With crowbars, wrenches, and metal shears, they pry open the door, release 65 from his buckles, and carry him to the recovery room.

They place the gurney on an examination table. The commander of the rescue team turns to one of his subordinates and tells him to call Bradley, who up to this point had been ordered to stand outside, into the room. Bradley approaches with hesitant steps. When the door opens, he pauses. A rescue team member places a hand on his shoulder, moving him forward to enter the room. He stands beside 65 and surveys the chimpanzee's exhausted face. 65 looks back at him, lifts his arms as if inviting Bradley to get closer, but then drops them to his sides and closes his eyes, surrendering to his fatigue. Bradley examines the open wound on the bridge of 65's nose. He lowers his head and brings one ear close to the ape's chest. His breathing is heavy. A technician hands him a pair of blunt-tipped scissors and he very carefully cuts open the spacesuit, first along the sleeves and then, cautious not to cut 65, along the body. The release of pressure eases 65's breathing. He raises his head and scans the room. Bradley looks at him with quiet care, then reaches out to him, brushing his fingers lightly over his matted fur. The chimpanzee doesn't flinch. Encouraged, Bradley gently strokes his head, his palm lingering over 65's brow as if reassuring him—you're safe now.

Their eyes meet. Bradley smiles, turns around, takes out of his bag a red apple, and offers it to 65. 65 holds out his large hand, grasps the apple, and brings it to his mouth. His cracked lips part as he bites through the peel, exposing the core of the fruit, and squeezes out the sweet juice from the apple's soft flesh. The juice is trickling between his teeth slipping down his chin. His parched throat gulps it down, but it is not enough. He bites again, harder this time, his lips pressing against the chilled fruit, rubbing against the rugged texture, drawing out every last drop. His eyelids grow heavy. His body relaxes. The last bit of apple slips from his weakening grasp and falls to the ground.

The technicians exchange glances, their work now done. With quiet efficiency, they gather their tools, and file out of the room. The door shuts behind them.

Bradley barely registers their departure. His focus remains on 65. He hesitates, then reaches for a soft tissue and gently dries 65's damp mouth. The chimpanzee does not react. Bradley's hand lingers, as if grounding himself in the moment. Then without thinking, as if not knowing what else to do, he drops to his knees. He gathers the fallen pieces of apple and sweeps away the wet stain from the laminate surface. The room is quiet now, save for the faint hum of machinery and the slow, even breaths of the ape beside him. Bradley exhales. His body feels heavy. Relief settles over him, pressing into his limbs, soft and undeniable. He rises to his feet, his body swaying slightly as exhaustion pulls at him. He crosses the room and sinks into a chair in the corner. He leans back and shuts his eyes.

65 is safe.

The thought drifts through his mind like mist after a violent storm.

But the peace doesn't last. A door clicks shut. The sharp finality of the sound slices through his haze, forcing his eyes open.

A veterinarian in a white coat is standing by the examination table. He leans over 65, slides an inflatable cuff over his arm and measures his blood pressure. Then he rests two fingers on 65's wrist and checks his pulse.

The veterinarian inclines his head in Bradley's direction

and asks him to come and help. Bradley steps forward and gently holds 65 down, pinning him to the mattress while murmuring to him soft reassuring words in a low and steady voice. The veterinarian carefully wipes away congealed blood from the chimpanzee's eyes with a damp cloth and carefully pulls back each eyelid, exposing each eye and shining an ophthalmoscope into it. 65 flinches, squirms, baring his teeth. For a moment, the veterinarian is startled and instinctively pulls back. Bradley doesn't hesitate, steps forward, reaches out to 65, and unfastens the soft padded straps. The ape responds immediately, climbing into Bradley's arms, wrapping his own arms around Bradley's chest and settling in his lap. The veterinarian leaves the room. Bradley looks around for a quiet corner. Sensing 65's thirst, he offers him a cup of water. 65 grasps the cup with both hands, gulping down the liquid quickly. Gradually, a sparkle reappears in the ape's eyes. He tightens his grip and hugs Bradley.

They are alone now, away from the crew members. The two of them sit together on a green plastic chair in a closed room at the ship's stern. Their chests move in tandem, they inhale and exhale, sharing the air that hangs between them in the empty room.

Bradley feels frustrated, but he's unsure why. Anger sabotages his thoughts. He remembers Dr. Kaine and how he used to frequently talk about the strange case of a Russian researcher named Ilya Ivanovich Ivanov, who became famous for artificial insemination methods in animals. Dr. Kaine developed an obsession regarding Ivanov's aspiration to create a human-ape hybrid. One day, Bradley asked Kaine why he thought the Soviet authorities had supported Ivanov, and he replied that, in his opinion, Stalin hoped that

Ivanov's success would enable the development of a breed of brave warriors with tremendous strength and underdeveloped brains. Dr. Kaine recounted that in 1926, Ivanov had received a grant from the Soviet regime and had sailed to Africa, to the Pasteur Institute in French Guinea. There he collected semen from African men and then inseminated it into the uteruses of three adult chimpanzees. After failing, he decided to try again, but this time he reversed the roles and tried to inseminate women with ape semen. He planned to perform these inseminations in a hospital in the Congo without the women's knowledge or consent, but when his intentions became known to local French medical authorities, they banned the experiment and forced him to leave.

In 1927 he returned to the Soviet Union with thirteen chimpanzees purchased from African animal traders. Most of the apes succumbed to the grueling journey and died along the way. He held those who survived in a research laboratory he established in Georgia. At the time, he received support from the Communist Academy, which was conducting experiments on fertilization of Soviet women for the purpose of improving the human race. He recruited a group of idealistic women for the study who agreed to undergo fertilization with chimpanzee semen and to relinquish any offspring.

He was forced to give up when the last male ape in his possession died. By this stage, Stalin's patience had run out. One day, without warning, two strangers knocked on the door of Ivanov's laboratory. A few minutes later, according to testimony from neighbors, he left the laboratory with them. The two men carried stacks of documents and papers, apparently gathered from Ivanov's work desk. He was never seen again. The remaining chimpanzees were transferred to a local zoo, and a veil of silence descended upon the laboratory.

THE VETERINARIAN KNOCKS on the door, enters, and informs Bradley that the helicopter is ready: they must return to the mothership. Bradley and 65 go up to the deck of the *Donner* and walk toward the cockpit. The noise of the propellers and the spray of salty water frighten 65, and he tries to break free from Bradley's hands. Bradley whispers in his ear, but his words are swept away by the wind, scattering over the vast sea. The ape pushes and scratches, wriggles in his arms, and almost falls. Bradley tightens his grip, asserting his authority, and firmly lifts him into the helicopter. The chopper takes off, and, finally, the ape relaxes. He looks around, strokes his chest hair, raises a finger to Bradley's forehead, and runs it along his eyebrows.

Bradley closes his eyes, reflecting on the day's events. He thinks about 65's turbulent flight, the splashdown of the Mercury-Redstone rocket into the Atlantic Ocean, and the absurdity of a chimp astronaut.

He thinks to himself, how different this day is from the ones that preceded it—how their world has been irrevocably shaken.

Tomorrow, 65's name will be emblazoned in all the newspaper headlines.

All of humanity will be in an uproar, but in the land of apes there will be silence.

The pilot signals that they are about to land. Bradley tightens his grip on 65. Through the window he sees the ground crew, their fluorescent vests glowing in the golden light of the setting sun, guiding the helicopter with illuminated red wands. The chopper descends steadily, the rotor blades slowing gradually until they come to a complete halt.

Neon tubes arranged in three rows across the ceiling cast a cold, sterile light over the examination room, emitting a monotonous hum that fills the space. Two veterinarians in white coats approach the chimpanzee, who is restrained on the glaring stainless steel table. One of the veterinarians shaves a spot on the ape's arm, ties a rubber tube around it, then takes a syringe and draws a clear liquid from a brown ampoule. He tilts the needle toward the ceiling, draining the air bubble and squeezing it out of the syringe. Then he rotates 65's wrist by 180 degrees, lowers it, and inserts the sharp needle into his arm. 65's face contorts as the cold liquid seeps through his bloodstream. His head becomes heavy, and he sinks into a deep sleep.

Bradley steps back. The veterinarians carry out the necessary tests, assessing cardiological functions and comparing values. One of them pulls out white gloves from a packet, blows into them, and slips his hands inside. The second veterinarian opens a narrow, long aluminum packet and passes a curved needle to his colleague. The veterinarian threads the needle through the edge of the wound and sutures the deep cut on the bridge of the nose. After finishing, he uses stainless steel forceps to wind the remaining thread. He pulls it taut, tightens it, and secures the ends on both sides of the cut. The two sides adhere to each other, and the bleeding wound is sealed. He applies an antibiotic ointment to the nose and covers it with a pad.

Bradley walks back to his room under a black sky. The

Milky Way stretches out above his head, pouring starlight over Earth. He raises his head and gazes up at the twinkling lights.

For a moment, he feels an urge to count them, but the thought that there are over two hundred billion stars overwhelms him, and he gives up. The stars lay bare his solitude, reminding him of summer vacations as a teenager when he went on hikes with his father to the Catskills and the green expanses of the Hudson River Valley. It was on these trips that his father taught him to ride a horse, build a tent, identify plants, observe birds, and track reptiles and mammals. It was on these trips that he learned to recognize the North Star, fixed above the horizon. He can still picture his father, standing and pointing, explaining in a velvety voice that Polaris is located directly above the Earth's rotation axis and promising it will always be right there, guiding him. "The light you're now seeing," he recalls him saying, "left the star four hundred and sixty years ago, and so, at this very moment, you're seeing the past in the present."

He remembers those words clearly—not just for their wonder, but for the deep impression they left on him, shaping the way he saw time, space, and his own place among the stars.

On another night, by the light of a bonfire, they sat alone in a forest clearing. His father read aloud a story about hunters, bears, and other animals carved like sculptures against the backdrop of trees and a wild landscape. The story told of the never-ending struggle for existence that defines nature, ordained by ancient rules, devoid of remorse, bereft of mercy.

BRADLEY CONTINUES WALKING alone, enters the trailer, goes into his room. Exhausted from the long day, he lies down on the bed and immediately falls asleep without undressing. In his dream, he walks alongside his father again, in the misty light of a fall morning. They make their way across an expansive meadow, among damp green and yellow grasses that jut out like tall spears bursting from the ground. Their feet trample the soil. The thick soles of their shoes crush the grass, sketching trails in the virginal prairie. His father removes the hunting rifle from his shoulder and hands it to Bradley. There is a rustle in the bushes, and they stop dead in their tracks. His father places a finger to his lips, motioning Bradley to stay silent, and then points to the rifle, gesturing to Bradley to raise the barrel and pull the bolt. Bradley presses the rifle's cold stock against the hollow of his shoulder and waits. The muscles in his arms tense, his half-closed eye fixed on the sight. They both stand there, their breathing quiet. Silence reigns over the moment. Bradley hears nothing but the pounding of his heart. His body stiffens and fills with dread. Only the shadow of his father's figure hovering above him prevents him from turning around and fleeing. Poised, he imagines the future about to unfold. And then suddenly, without warning, a sharp rustle is heard. From among the grasses, a small flock of gray partridges emerges. They are red-beaked, their eyes accentuated by a thick black line. He jerks back, colliding with his father, who places a hand on his shoulder and whispers to him in a firm tone to squeeze the trigger. Without thinking, he does as he is told. A single blast rips through the silence, and at the same time his heart cries, No!

It is too late.

The recoil drives the rifle's hard stock against his collar bone and, immediately after, the sound of flapping wings disturbs the blades of wild grass. Three frightened birds take flight, pushing the air with their mottled wings, soaring upward, fleeing for their lives. A plumage of feathers, both light and azure, scatter in the air, sketching lines of farewell to the bird left behind, lying on the cold earth.

Afterward, silence.

The smell of sulfur fills Bradley's nostrils. His mouth is dry and a metallic taste lingers on his tongue. Bradley and his father approach the dead bird, the one chosen by the bullet. They crouch over it. He places his hand on the contracted chest, gently stroking the feathers, which are soft to the touch. His hand trembles, and he flinches. The bird's body is still warm. He dips his finger into the pool of blood and notices a swarm of ants drawing near. He inhales deeply, absorbing the mixture of sulfureous fumes and blood, the acrid scent of death he had not imagined until that moment.

His father grabs the partridge by the legs, swinging it into the air. The bird's limp, ruddy neck droops down and sways from side to side. The three of them retreat without saying a word. The bird's blood seeps into the earth. In another moment, there will be no trace left of the pivotal instant when the bird's life met a bullet. A deathly silence takes over the green landscape, stifling the song of the forest birds.

BRADLEY AWAKES, TERRIFIED, and sits up in bed. He removes a cigarette from his shirt pocket, lights it, and smokes slowly, bitterness searing his tongue. After a few drags, he crushes the cigarette butt between his fingers and lies down on his back. He tosses and turns restlessly from side to side, and finally goes back to sleep.

He awakens to sunshine penetrating the closed shutters. Strips of light divide his body into orderly geometric shapes, right-angled rectangles imposing themselves on his lanky, rounded body. His head is heavy, his hair stands on end, suffused with a negative electrical charge. He sits on the edge of the mattress, motionless, allowing the sun to thaw his heart, frozen from the night's tribulations. A few minutes later he gets to his feet, puts on his glasses, and slowly shuffles off to the bathroom. He stands in front of the mirror, looking at himself, horrified at the sight of his ashen face. He blinks, trying to filter the intrusive light through his lashes. He lowers his head, turns on the faucet, removes his glasses, fills his cupped hands with water, and plunges into the cold reflection staring back at him.

Afterward, he brushes his teeth meticulously, polishing them with dedication, moving methodically from tooth to tooth, following the gum line. He pays attention to the gaps between his teeth, maneuvering the bristles into the crevices. His hand and toothbrush work efficiently, moving back and forth in cyclic motions, hoping to defend the sturdy yet helpless teeth from the relentless attacks of a stubborn army of bacteria that constantly threatens to drill through the protective walls, crumble the enamel, and wreak havoc.

He replaces the toothbrush, rinses his mouth again, and removes his clothes, folding each item and placing it on a wooden bench next to the shower. He steps naked into the bathtub and washes his body, surrendering to the flow of hot water. He scrubs his skin with a cracked bar of soap, closes his eyes, and retraces his steps from bed to bathroom. In his imagination, he draws all the landmarks he encountered along the way—the crease marks his body left on the sheet, the work pants discarded by the bed, the slippers peeking out, abandoned under the mattress. In his mind, he stitches together fragments of memories, striving to paint an image of the dead partridge, struggling to immortalize the expressionless face and empty gaze that stared out from those black eyes and the fragile, limp body. It was so long ago, but when he thinks about it, everything comes back to him as if it were only yesterday. Despite the fact that since then everyone who was there and everything that was there has vanished, died, or gone away, and nothing is the same.

He imagines the frozen body of the dead bird, covered in a down of silvery and ruddy feathers, whispering to him. A voice that wraps the entire cosmos in delicate cobwebs, eternal and omnipresent, hovering above both the living and the dead. This vision, though devoid of language, speaks to him and reminds him that there are things that do not change.

He ponders the life he has chosen and wonders if perhaps it is rather this life that has chosen him. This thought sweeps him away, unchecked, and finally stops as the hot water runs out. He turns off the tap, grabs a white towel, and dries himself off. He puts on his glasses, examines the reddish stubble in the mirror, and covers his face with shaving cream. With a fresh razor he shaves carefully until his skin is clean and no stubble remains. He wipes the leftover foam and splashes his face with aftershave. He spreads a towel on a chair in front of the writing desk, sits down, opens the black notebook, and begins to transform his dream into words. Like a painter insisting on precision in shades, he writes down the image of his father who came to visit him on his thirteenth birthday, holding a stuffed partridge. The silvery bird was plump and stiff, skewered on a metal rod that protruded from a rectangular wooden base painted black. He describes his father's facial features: his smile, the taut lips, the prominent cheekbones that softened his stiff expression and emphasized the mischievous glimmer in his eyes. He weaves fragments of memory into a chain of events that flash through his mind like a sequence of photographs merging into one another, appearing and disappearing.

The writing exhausts him. He stops, places the pen on the wooden surface, closes the notebook, gets dressed, and leaves the room.

*　*　*

BRADLEY STANDS THERE LOOKING AT THE APE, OBSERVING 65 through the bars, watching him as he gazes at the ceiling with glazed eyes.

Bradley opens the cage door. 65 rushes out, runs toward him and jumps into his arms. Bradley hugs him, carefully removes the bandage from his nose, and peeks at the sutures. The skin has closed over the cut, the edges of the wound now sealed together, leaving behind a thin line of dried blood as sole reminder of the incision.

He goes to the refrigerator and takes out a cocktail of strawberries, blueberries, and antibiotic fluid diluted with sweet raspberries. At the sight of the drink, 65 licks his lips, takes the cup in his hand, and empties it in one gulp. It is 08:32 AM. In two hours, they are due to appear before a crowd of journalists and photographers gathered from all corners of the country to meet, hear, and commemorate the story of the chimpanzee who returned to Earth from a star-studded sky. Bradley dreads this moment. He watches apprehensively as the ape licks the remains of the berry puree with gusto.

He goes over to 65 and picks him up, removing the empty cup from his hand. They begin walking toward the dining room. After about three hundred feet, he lowers 65 to the ground, and they continue onward, hand in hand, toward the hazy horizon. Bradley walks at an even pace, but 65's legs are weak, and his knees buckle as he struggles to maintain his balance. Bradley stops, bends down and scoops up 65 again, and they continue on their way.

They sit alone in the dining room. On the table is a bowl of cornflakes soaked in milk, a plate of scrambled eggs, home fries, and a few strips of bacon. Bradley squeezes condensed milk from a metal tube onto a round silver spoon and hands it to the ecstatic ape, who quickly licks the spoon clean of the thick, sweet mixture. Once finished, 65 hands the gleaming spoon back to Bradley, beseeching him for more with his eyes. Bradley tries to divert his attention and pushes the bowl of cornflakes toward the ape. But 65 refuses to give up. He tips over the bowl, spills the milk, pounds his fist on the table, and screeches. Bradley relinquishes his fork, succumbing to the chimpanzee's furious onslaught, and hands over the tube of condensed milk. The chimp calms down instantaneously, puts the nozzle in his mouth, and sucks the remaining milk with the smug satisfaction of a champ.

*   *   *

IT IS JUST THE TWO OF THEM IN THE ROOM NOW. THE CHIMP plays on the bed, wrestling with the bedclothes, playing hide and seek, pulling the blanket, diving under it, and reappearing among the white sheets. Bradley gazes out the window. He notices a small, lively bird hopping on the branches of a low scrub oak bush. He goes over to the nightstand and picks up the *Peterson Field Guide to Birds*. Returning to the window to look at the bird, he notes its black back, the dark stripes crossing its chest, the long tail feathers, and the rounded, seed-eating beak and above it a crescent of sandy plumage around the eyes. The bird flutters its wings. It is clearly a sparrow, and on closer examination, he determines with certainty that it is a Dusky Seaside Sparrow. Its song, he reads, is unique due to its remote habitat, which isolates the bird from similar species and family members. He further learns that it nests among grasses growing on the banks of brackish water lakes. Most of its kind have perished as collateral damage in the ongoing war between humans and mosquitoes. The sparrows are the unintended victims of this war. Even the missile base is routinely sprayed with toxic chemicals every summer. He follows the bird with his eyes. It is beautiful, completely unaware of the danger, foraging for food in a minefield. Suddenly, the bird takes a few small hops back, and Bradley thinks the bird has noticed him. He watches the bird as it moves away, advancing in light hops along the branch before soaring away, dissolving into the velvety softness of the skies.

He turns his head and sees the chimp lying on the bed, curled up in a cloud of white shrouds.

* * *

FOLLOWING THE EXTENSIVE MEDIA COVERAGE AND 65'S
new public status, Edward Black, Holloman's public relations
officer, raises concerns that the program's functional-instru-
mental attitude toward the chimpanzees, and the fact they
have no names, could be perceived as inhumane and damage
the laboratory's image. Hamilton Garbinsky, the general in
charge of the Biological Research Unit, agrees. He, too, fears
that the consequences could be damaging, that it could cause
the public to doubt the value of the program and might even
impact future funding. He summons his subordinates to an
urgent meeting and announces that the monkeys must be
given names. After hours of animated discussion and debate,
Black suggests giving them biblical names; maybe the names
of prophets would work, he adds. At first, his proposal is met
with ridicule. The committee members think it is a joke, and
only Hamilton Garbinsky keeps quiet. Then Garbinsky calls
for silence, turns to Edward, and asks him to prepare a list
of possible names.

*   *   *

A KNOCK AT THE DOOR DISRUPTS THEIR TRANQUILITY. 65
awakens from his nap and quickly jumps off the bed. He
clings to Bradley, wrapping his arms tightly around Bradley's
thigh. At the door stands Henry Jones, the Air Force's public
relations officer. They exchange a few short sentences. Henry
briefs Bradley on how to present the astrochimp to the press.
Outside, it is very noisy. Dozens of reporters and news photographers are jostling together, beyond the fence.

Intimidated by the commotion, 65 blinks, turns his head
away, and climbs over Bradley's shoulder, then jumps down,

and takes refuge behind Bradley's back.

Henry turns around and addresses the crowd, calling them to order, but everyone ignores him, stampeding the gate and rushing toward the chimpanzee. Henry gives Bradley a quick look, signals him to lift the ape into his arms, and simultaneously steps in front of them in an attempt to shield 65 with his body. He turns to the crowd again, warning them in an authoritative tone, but to no avail; his voice is drowned by the roars of a frenzied mob.

Bradley pulls 65 closer to him, sensing the chimpanzee's anxiety. 65's fur bristles, he curls his upper lip, wrinkles his mottled nose, and bares his teeth with a threatening snarl. Bradley tries to restrain him, fearing he might lose control. 65's body sways nervously from side to side, his head jerking back and forth as if possessed.

The crowd closes in on them; the cameras flash incessantly. Bradley turns his back on the crowd and retreats into the trailer. He shuts the door. The wooden barrier muffles the noise of the crowd. Silence descends upon the room. He leans against the door, tightly hugging 65, caressing the back of his neck and speaking to him softly. They stand there, motionless, their bodies intertwined like a tightly woven braid. The warmth of Bradley's body curled around 65 instills a sense of security in 65, and his composure gradually returns.

A sharp knock on the door ruptures the silence, like a small earthquake, a jolt that releases the moment from the spring that held it. Immediately after, Henry's voice can be heard from the other side of the door. Bradley cautiously opens the door and steps out.

This time, the journalists and the photographers practice

restraint. Henry introduces Bradley, who in turn presents the chimpanzee known until now as 65, by his new name: Ham.

As he mutters the name through his teeth, he feels the air heating up again. Bradley senses how Ham's hair follicles stiffen, how his fur bristles and causes him to puff up. He senses the vibrating air molecules, colliding with each other in disturbed disarray. And suddenly, without warning, like a wave of kinetic energy, the photographers erupt again. Flashes from cameras blind Ham, and his face contorts into a grimace that appears through the glass lenses as an endearing smile.

Gray clouds pass overhead, obscuring hues of the blue in the sky.

The photographers snap relentlessly, drowning Ham's contorted and anxious grimace in an ocean of silver halides.

Tomorrow, he will be famous. A photograph of him will appear in newspapers, accompanied by sensational head-lines. Millions of people around the world will read about him, captivated by what appears to be his mischievous smile, which will seem to them so human, and so sweet.

The photographers, like sorcerers, transform Ham into a mute image preserved on film, sentencing him to silence. Even the anguished cry now ripped from his throat is silenced, as his image is captured on the celluloid surface, scorched by light. After photographing from every possi-ble angle, the photographers finally lose interest, turn their backs, and walk away.

The sudden lull soothes Bradley and, for a moment, he feels relief. Ham remains anxious. His terrified smile dis-appears, but he continues to tap his feet and rock his body back and forth. Bradley tries to reassure him but then, in an instant, Ham breaks free from Bradley's arms and bolts. Bradley raises his voice, orders him to stay put, but the chimp lurches forward, his knuckles stretching ahead, barely skimming the ground as his powerful legs propel him forward. He moves in sharp bursts—zigzagging, bounding, twisting. Bradley chases after him, but Ham's speed is too great for Bradley to match. Dust rises in his wake, swallowing his small frame until he vanishes completely. Exhausted, Bradley stops. He catches his breath and resumes his search. His legs feel heavy, but he continues striding toward the ape's enclosure, thinking that perhaps Ham has run back home, to his cage. When he does not find him, he stands still and begins calling out his name. Guilt and inadequacy weigh on him as he wanders aimlessly in the quiet missile launch base. Finally, he sinks to the ground beneath a large sycamore tree growing beside the fence on the southern border of the camp. He draws his knees up to his chest and hugs them, allowing his chin to rest on his knees. He stares at the roots of the tree, thick roots that run into the heart of the earth. A sound distracts him from his thoughts. He raises his head but sees nothing and assumes it's just the leaves rustling in the evening breeze. The sound persists. Bradley raises his head again and scans the dense canopy of the tree. He follows the sound; although he still can't see anything, he continues to search. And then, to his surprise, he notices a pair of eyes, glowing orange, on a high branch, staring down at him. He stands up and steps back, improving his vantage point. From there, he can clearly see long, ear-like feathers protruding from both sides of a head and a brown belly covered with pale spots. He identifies it immediately: It is a long-eared owl. He knows these owls migrate here during the winter months, but because they are shy and mostly active at dusk, only a few people are lucky enough to see them. The owl does not linger; it averts its gaze, spreads its wings, and flies away. Bradley continues to follow it with his eyes as it soars and rises skyward, carried by a warm air current before disappearing into the blur of twilight. He walks along the camp fence, wandering aimlessly. But just when he is about to give up, he spots Ham near the fence. The chimp is sitting alone under a thick, gray concrete wall, withdrawn into himself, quietly watching a group of seagulls hovering in the sky. The cool ocean breeze tousles his fur, and after the flock of seagulls disperses, Ham lowers his eyes to the ground and stares at the sand.

Bradley hesitates for a moment, watching Ham from a distance, and then approaches very slowly. Ham notices him but does not move from where he is sitting. When Bradley is just a few steps away from him, he pauses, whispers Ham's name, bends down, extends one hand in Ham's direction and then takes another step. Finally, he is close enough to gently touch the chimp's head.

Ham recoils, closing up like the petals of a flower at nightfall. Bradley drops to his knees and wraps his arms around him. Ham surrenders to the warmth of his embrace, and Bradley feels the chimp wilting in his arms.

Above the horizon, the sun blazes, painting the skies in glowing hues of orange, yellow, purple, and crimson. Bradley stares at the spectacular light show and wonders if the skies are painted with such intensity because of a distant volcano eruption. Perhaps intense heat from the earth's depths is now rushing toxic gases to the heavens. He imagines the colors of methane, nitrogen, fluoric acids, sulfur, and magnesium scattering blue light in the air and blurring the glow of the setting sun.

Or perhaps, he thinks, the skies are glowing due to a nuclear test. As he contemplates the searing hues, a shiver runs through him, and he tightens his hold of the chimp. Ham's ruffled fur rubs against Bradley's face, and he inhales the acidic scent emanating from it. He places a finger under Ham's chin, lifts his head, and gazes into his amber eyes. The air settles, darkness falls upon the camp, and the day's events dissolve into stars. Bradley feels a certain relief, rises to his feet, takes hold of the chimpanzee's hand, and together they walk back to the trailer.

When they arrive, Bradley opens the cage door, and Ham acquiesces, crawling inside and stretching out on the straw mattress. Bradley covers him with a military flannel blanket, and Ham pulls it over its head and curls up, seeking security. Bradley sits in the darkness and watches him, mulling over the press conference and the desperate attempts of the photographers to capture Ham. No photograph, he thinks, can truly capture a living creature.

When Ham falls asleep, Bradley gets up from his seat and quietly leaves the room.

*　　*　　*

THE NEXT MORNING, THEY FLEW BACK TO THE CHIMPANZEE colony at the Holloman Air Force Base in New Mexico. The day passed slowly. It was a banal day, a blank page in Bradley's memory. At Holloman, the veterinarians and team of scientists came out to greet them. Everyone was excited, hugging each other and shaking hands. At the chimpanzee colony, all the chimpanzees crowded around Ham.

* * *

THE NEXT DAY, A SERIES OF FOLLOW-UP TESTS BEGAN. Veterinarians examined the physiological and psychological effects of the flight on Ham's body and mind. A technical malfunction in the missile launch had slightly altered the angle of ascent, exposing Ham to immense forces of gravitational acceleration. Ionizing cosmic radiation emitted from the sun and distant galactic sources penetrated his body and broke atomic bonds between electrons and nucleus. Cells were destroyed, molecules changed their composition, and it was possible that a genetic accident had manifested itself in his chromosomes.

Could the space flight have altered his genetic hereditary structural encoder? Could the space flight have rendered him sterile? Or perhaps the opposite, was Ham destined to bring a new breed of chimpanzees into the world?

* * *

THE DAYS PASSED, BUT NOT LIKE BEFORE.

Ham was withdrawn. Bradley tried to cheer him up by offering plates laden with bananas, grapes, apples, and pieces of coconut. Ham, however, remained apathetic. The chimp refused to cooperate, even when Bradley took him for walks in the woods to the south of the base and tried to play hide-and-seek. After three days, Bradley changed his approach. He visited him every morning and read stories to him from books he borrowed from the local library in Cocoa Beach, which he visited on weekends. He became friendly with Diana Bayer, a librarian who worked there. She had approached Bradley after recognizing him from a newspaper article. She was very interested in Ham, and Bradley listened to her and answered all her questions patiently. It was her idea to read to Ham. She asked if he had ever tried telling Ham stories. He took Rudyard Kipling's *The Jungle Book* out of the library and began reading passages to Ham about Mowgli, Bagheera, and Baloo. To his astonishment, Ham sat and listened to him intently whenever he spoke about the jungle. It seemed to Bradley that a spark of life ignited in Ham's eyes. From time to time, Bradley raised his head from the book and gazed into the eyes of this domesticated wild creature, as if seeking a glimmer of hope in the body and soul of the chimp who regarded him as a stranger since his flight into space.

*   *   *

DURING THE SPACE RACE, HUNDREDS OF THOUSANDS OF Americans functioned as cogs in a well-oiled machine. They drilled, they sweated, they developed and perfected an array of ballistic missiles. And in the Soviet Union, hundreds of thousands more fed another well-oiled machine.

Suspicion lies at the heart of fear, compelling people to keep secrets, stay vigilant, and observe one another closely. Fear possesses an inexplicable, almost magnetic power that draws people together, forming unexpected connections and fostering a strange closeness. For that reason, a profound intimacy may sometimes be shared between enemies.

In some ways, the relationship between enemies can be similar to that of passionate lovers.

Sergei Pavlovich Korolev, the head of the Soviet space program, and Wernher von Braun, the brain behind the American project, were such a couple—mutually enamored enemies who dreamed of each other at night.

In the middle of the night, Korolev woke up in a sweat at Baikonur, the Soviet missile base in Kazakhstan. He was troubled by a butterfly that appeared in his dream, a butterfly with white wings, decorated with brown and gray specks and dots. The colors were patterned like a delicate system of veins carved on rare marble. He watched the butterfly as it fluttered along, flying among mustard flowers in yellow and orange ochre, darting with alacrity from one flower to another, inserting its long tongue into the fertile flower ovaries. For reasons he couldn't explain, von Braun lingered in his thoughts, tied to the dream. The space project had fused their fates, binding them like Siamese twins. The thought offered no comfort, only an unsettling sense of inevitability.

Korolev admired von Braun, yet longed to destroy him, to be the first to develop a missile that would fly into space and orbit Earth. He believed this goal was within reach. He calculated the forces of gravity and countered them with the centripetal force. According to Newton's laws, he knew that if these two forces were perfectly balanced, gravity would pull the missile toward Earth, but its velocity would be sufficient to offset the fall, allowing it to continue its arced trajectory and maintain a stable orbit around the planet.

He feared, however, that von Braun would beat him to it. America was the richest country in the world and he believed that von Braun had far more resources at his disposal. He scoured American scientific journals and general life-style magazines, meticulously trawling through them in the hope of finding a clue. He had heard about Ham and seen the photo of him on the cover of *Life*.

Nina, his secretary, translated the article for him. She was the one who told him the chimpanzee's name, that he had been sent into space in a Mercury-Redstone rocket and that there was much excitement in America because, physically and mentally, the ape was almost human. In fact, she added, the chimpanzee's mission was a dress rehearsal for human space flight; the capsule and the life-support systems were almost identical to those that would carry astronauts into orbit.

The magazine was filled with impressive photos. He studied them intently—images of chimps, scientists, and medical and technical equipment. He let the visuals seep into his mind, feeding his consciousness with a mix of thoughts, hopes, and fears. Ham's eyes, though expressionless, carried a haunting depth, striking Korolev as profoundly human. He immersed himself in the photograph, examining Ham's shaved torso, tracing the electrical wires wrapped around his abdomen and thighs, the electrodes attached to his chest and groin.

In the nights that followed, Korolev was unable to shake off Ham's image from his mind. "I never attach importance to dreams," he said to Nina, "but I can't get this monkey out of my head." She looked at him but said nothing. He didn't elaborate, just lowered his gaze and took a sip of black coffee from a mug.

Over lunch, he and Nina discussed a series of articles published by von Braun in *Collier's*. They analyzed every word, examining diagrams like photographs. And almost imperceptibly, through the time the two of them spent poring over the various articles about Ham, she became Korolev's lover.

In bed at night, Nina read to Korolev a quote from von Braun in which he claimed humanity was on the brink of a revelation: "This is not science fiction. In the near future a manned space station will be established, and the country that achieves this will dominate the world. From the space station, it will be possible to observe everything happening on earth, and the space station may also serve as a platform for launching nuclear missiles. The space station will orbit the Earth at a speed of 18,000 miles per hour, and whoever controls it will be capable of imposing their will on the human race, to bring peace or tyranny to the world."

The Soviets forced Korolev to live in obscurity. They kept him as a closely guarded secret, lest he be harmed. Few knew his identity. In public, he had no name; in the press, they referred to him as the Chief Designer.

But CIA agents made sure von Braun knew everything about him. He knew that in his youth, Korolev's parents had divorced, and that after his father left home, his mother, Maria Nikolaevna Balanina, had entrusted him to his grandmother. He knew that Korolev had trained as an aeronautical engineer, that he had been accused of crimes he did not commit, that Stalin had sentenced him to hard labor in the Kolyma gold mines of Siberia. He knew everything about him, down to the exact number of teeth Korolev had lost due to malnutrition in the Gulag.

The Cold War defined them. The space race gave each of them an identity and a purpose. They needed each other. Von Braun was dependent on Korolev, and Korolev could not exist without von Braun. Bradley and Ham were similarly trapped in a web of secrets, without either of them realizing it—a web spun by Eisenhower and Khrushchev, and by the world's relentless drive for progress.

✳   ✳   ✳

IN 1957, ABOUT A MONTH AFTER LAUNCHING THE FIRST satellite, the Soviets dealt another blow to American morale by launching Sputnik 2 into space, this time carrying a small mongrel dog named Laika. Although Laika was burned alive by the heat of the compressors immediately after takeoff, she will always be remembered as the first dog to orbit the Earth.

The humiliation of yet another defeat made the Americans realize that the real competition was over who would be the first to send a human being to the moon. They carefully selected seven astronauts, superheroes who became known as the "Mercury Seven," named after the rocket that would carry them. The Soviets, working feverishly on a similar project, maintained strict secrecy, keeping their chosen cosmonauts anonymous.

On April 12, 1961, three weeks before the scheduled launch of Alan Shepard, the senior astronaut of the Mercury Seven, the Americans suffered a most painful blow—Yuri Gagarin, a Russian cosmonaut whose name had only recently been revealed, completed a full orbit around the Earth and became the first man in space.

A week later, the Americans faced yet another defeat. This time on the ground, at the Bay of Pigs, on the Cuban coast of Girón. An army of Cuban exiles, trained by the Americans, failed in their attempt to ignite a popular uprising and overthrow Fidel Castro's socialist regime in Cuba. The young, recently elected President John F. Kennedy understood that these repeated defeats at the hands of the Soviets demanded a bold response. In an historic speech to the nation, he pledged to land a man on the moon by the end of the 1960s, and to bring him safely back to earth.

*   *   *

A MISSIVE WAS SENT TO THE BASE ANNOUNCING THE decision to delay the flight of astronaut John Glenn, originally scheduled to take off and orbit the Earth in a Mercury-Atlas rocket. NASA's command headquarters resolved to minimize risks by conducting another test flight with a chimp. "This time," Hamilton Garbinsky announced to the training crew, "it will be a far more complex mission."

Ham, Enos, Elisha, and Zechariah were chosen for the operation. For a month, they underwent relentless training, at the end of which only one of the four would be selected. In this launch, the chosen chimp would be sent beyond the atmosphere to orbit the Earth three times.

Training began that very day. Enos and Ham were strapped into a capsule inside a heavy steel simulator. Ham tried to resist, so they locked him inside the capsule until he calmed down. Every hour, they opened the door to check his condition and offered him food and water. After twelve hours, they released him, cleaned the capsule of feces and urine, and provided more food and water. Once he calmed down, they instructed Bradley to return him to the training facility. This time, Ham no longer dared resist physically. Nonetheless, Bradley still could hear him howling as the simulator began to rotate. Gravitational forces crushed Ham's body, nearly causing him to choke on the accumulated acids in his throat. His eyes sunk deep into their sockets, as if his skull was about to shatter. After a few minutes, when the crew were no longer sure if Ham was still conscious, they gradually reduced the speed of the carousel until it creaked to a halt. Another minute passed before the technician and Bradley approached. The technician opened the door. Ham lay motionless, his eyes closed. Bradley knelt beside him, wiped his lips with a cloth, and dried the mucus that stained his fur.

Training recommenced after lunch. This time, Enos tried to resist. He conceded defeat after being zapped by an electric shocker.

The four chimpanzees were taught fifty words in sign language and what to do in response to seeing certain shapes and colors. They were strapped with leather restraints to small metal chairs in front of computer screens displaying light sequences in red, blue, white, and green.

Enos and Ham sat upright, facing the flashing light consoles. They were tasked with pulling levers according to the changing colors. Ham had to choose between two red circles and a green triangle. He hesitated, his finger hovering over the buttons. Bradley followed intently as Ham's heart pounded away. The chimp was expected to act quickly but he struggled to decide which lever to pull, and finally chose the red circle. Right away, a grating beep sounded, signaling an error, followed by a muffled yelp as the electric shock penetrated his foot. Then, silence. The smell of singed flesh lingered in the air. The lights went out. Ham curled up like a ball of wool. Bradley moved closer and spoke to him in a confident and reassuring voice, trying to encourage him. Ham ignored Bradley at first, but Bradley persisted, tapping gently on the window with a white writing board, urging Ham to continue. Reluctant at first, Ham eventually responded to Bradley's entreaties. After a minute, the colored lights came on again, exploding in his eyes like electrified stardust. Fear and thirst whispered to him that this time he must not err and, quickly, he pressed the green triangle. An encouraging beep was heard, followed by a yellow banana pellet shot straight into his mouth from a narrow metal tube that protruded at a right angle from a telescopic container that descended from the ceiling. With great agility, he caught the pellet between his lips, rolled it between his teeth, and dissolved it under his tongue. But his thirst gave him no rest. He tried to break free from the leather restraints. The lights turned on again, and once more he reacted swiftly, pressing the two green circles and immediately after, the blue square. Again, a beep sounded, indicating that he had successfully cracked the code. This time a butterfly valve opened, and water gushed directly into his mouth from a wide tube. He pressed his lips around the spout and eagerly sucked the sweet water.

The training session was over. Bradley released Ham, half-lifted him out of the chair, and led him back to his cage.

*   *   *

In the dining room, Bradley ate with Ralph Brady, the in-house photographer for *Life* magazine. Ralph had dedicated himself to the space project and frequently visited the ape colony. He felt deep affection for Ham and asked how he was doing. He told Bradley that his documentation of Ham's journey into space had received an overwhelming response and that the magazine's editorial office had been flooded with letters from enthusiastic readers.

Bradley described the new training regimen, designed to prepare the chimps for the complex missions ahead of them. Ralph asked if it would be possible for him to cover this next phase of the mission, too.

Bradley nodded in approval and replied that he did not see a problem.

Ralph continued enthusiastically. "It's stunning," he said. "When I watch you working together, it's like your body language merges, and you and the ape function as a single entity."

At the end of the meal, Ralph took out a black, worn leather binder from his briefcase. The thick binder, secured with a simple metal zipper, contained a collection of black-and-white photographs and a file of color photos relating to issues he had worked on.

Ralph sifted through the photographs and handed over a selection. Bradley wiped the table with a napkin and placed the photographs on the linoleum surface. He leaned forward, rested on his elbows, and examined the photographs carefully. These photographs, he thought, were like time capsules—a compressed version of the past folded into the present, disrupting all sense of continuity. The photographs drew Bradley in, disconnecting him from Ralph and the dinner time commotion. He took one print in his hands, moving the silvery resin-coated paper from side to side, his eyes following the shifting reflections. Light and shadow charged the frozen moments with visual tension.

Straightening briefly, he looked up and told Ralph that the photographs were wonderful. Then he turned back, lingering on a particular image of himself and Ham during a break in training. In this photograph the chimp clings to Bradley's thigh, his head tilted upward, eyes fixed on Bradley, who looms above him. Their gazes intersect, forever captured in the moment before the aperture snapped shut. To Bradley, it felt as though these tiny fragments of information had been resurrected, breaking free of the frame, hovering wildly in space—as if he could actually feel them, drilling into his mind and flooding the corridors of memory. He could not take his eyes off the photograph. He stared at the expression on the chimpanzee's face, which looked so much like a smile, and suddenly the visual lie was exposed. In this photograph, he thought, anxiety and madness had concealed their true identity

He felt a strange tingling in his fingertips, like a worm gnawing at him from the inside, nibbling beneath his skin. He held in his hand the February 1961 issue of *Life*. On the cover, Ham lay on his back inside the coffin-like flight capsule. The chimp's hands were folded across his chest, and his eyes were closed. His face appeared to be suffused with the serenity of an enlightened cult leader. He read the caption at the bottom of the photograph, written in small white letters: "Back from Space: A Confident Ham."

The photograph reminded him of the final scene from *Freaks,* an old, black-and-white circus film he had seen it years ago at the Rialto on the corner of 42nd Street and Broadway. While in high school, he used to slip away from classes to visit the movie theater. There, in the pitch-black auditorium, Bradley spent long hours watching one movie after another, from noon until sunset. The films were like a drug to him, blurring the boundaries between reality and illusion.

Now he was back there, in a back row at the Rialto, imagining himself watching the beautiful, lithe Cleopatra in *Freaks*. She was the circus trapeze queen who seduces the wealthy midget, Hans, into marrying her. In the wedding scene, a crowd of outcasts, amputees, Siamese twins, and deformed dwarfs host a wild feast in her honor. At the height of the evening, the guests burst into repeated cheers of revelry: "One of us, you're now one of us." They pass around a large goblet containing a potion, inviting everyone to drink from it. Cleopatra, who married not for love but out of greed, shudders and spits the potion in the face of a frenzied dwarf. At that moment, the crowd falls silent: The lie is exposed, and they cast her out from their midst. In a horrifying final scene, Cleopatra pays for her sin. Through sorcery, the grotesque creatures cut out her tongue, shorten her arms, tar her lower body, cover it with feathers, and thus turn her into a monstrous goose.

To shake this memory, Bradley quickly lifted his head, gave it a sharp shake, and took a deep breath. Pretending to appear calm, he thanked Ralph for sharing the photographs with him and apologized for not feeling well. Ralph sensed his distress, asked if he was okay, if he needed help, but Bradley politely declined. He got up from his chair and dragged himself toward the door. He made his way shakily through the darkness to the ape enclosure, under the glow of a crescent moon in a velvety night sky.

Bradley opened the door cautiously. He entered on tiptoe and sat down in a corner of the room. His eyes gradually adjusted to the dark, milking shadows out of the gloom. He recognized Ham's dark body mass. A curled up black stain, nestled in the golden straw mattress that he had carefully prepared for himself, as chimps do every night before sleep. Ham lay on his side in a spoon position, his right arm tucked under his head, his left arm hugging his chest. Bradley followed the steady rise and fall movements of his rib cage, the fluttering of his eyelids. He stared at him intently, as if trying to enter the chimp's salty dreams. He breathed deeply, drawing in the aroma of sweet hay and the scent of the sleeping ape. It felt warm in the cell. Steam rose from the water in the drinking bowl, escaping its liquid form, transforming into vapor, and filling the space around them with a faint haze.

*   *   *

IN THE MORNING, THEY TOOK HAM AND ENOS FOR TRAINING on the rocket sled. The sled's front section housed a seat, while its rear contained the engine of a ballistic missile. When activated, the sled hurtled forward at speeds of six hundred miles per hour before coming to an abrupt halt. The sudden braking was violent, like the impact of invisible rocks falling from the sky with the immense force of 30 Gs, crashing upon the passengers' heads. Each time the vehicle braked, the intense deceleration ruptured blood vessels in the eyes, causing subconjunctival hemorrhage, which led to a burning sensation and sometimes even temporary loss of vision.

The sled's ejection seats were developed by an engineer named Edward Murphy, a man known for his fiery temper. Whenever one of his experiments failed, Murphy would lash out at crew members. His volatile demeanor made him feared by the technicians, whose only resort was to quietly mock him behind his back. In a famous experiment he conducted with Dr. John Stapp, Murphy's collaborator on the sled project, disaster struck. The sled's carriage detached from the track, flew into the air, and erupted in flames. Murphy turned on the electrician responsible. "If there's more than one way to do a job," he yelled at him, "and one of them will end in disaster, you'll choose it."

Behind his back, his accusations became a joke. The quoted sentence stuck with the workers onsite like the plague and later became famous, known as Murphy's Law, in which anything that can go wrong—will go wrong.

Murphy's Law was etched on Ham's flesh.

Bradley looked at him; he seemed exhausted and shattered. But Hamilton Garbinsky insisted on continuing the training and not giving up.

*   *   *

IN THE MIDDLE OF THE NIGHT, BRADLEY AWOKE WITH AN urge to take Ham and escape. He had no plan, nor did he know where to go.

He sat on the bed and took a swig from the bottle of Johnnie Walker on his nightstand.

He lay on his back and tried to go back to sleep. His head was dizzy. Time, he felt, was whirling around him in circles, the seasons merging into each other, and his entire life condensed into a single moment that contained everything. His nostrils filled with scents of winter, immediately dissipated to merge with the perfumes of spring, followed by the deadly barrenness of summer. He found himself in a strange place, riding on horseback with his father. From a distance, he saw two children fighting among ruined houses, and heard the echoing sound of barking dogs in the background. They rode through empty streets. Among the ruins, random kitchen utensils and pieces of furniture lay covered in moss. Suddenly his mother appeared, walking toward them. He stopped his horse and reached out to her. As he drew closer, her appearance changed—she no longer looked like his mother. She was now a mythological hairy creature with the tapered ears of a satyr. She kissed his cheek and whispered for him to close his eyes. He obeyed. His head grew heavy, and he began to drift off. But then, a tremor shook him, followed by a dull thud. He lifted his head and saw his father lying on the floor, blood oozing from his head. He tried to call his mother, desperate for help, but she was no longer there. The two of them were alone again in the fields, surrounded by an endless expanse of grass. Night fell. In the distance, the howls of coyotes could be heard. Above them, the sky glowed with stars. He raised his eyes and gazed at the vast basket of universe spread above his head. He searched for the North Star, unable to fathom where it had disappeared to. And then, it suddenly struck him that the thud that had shaken him was not his father's fall, but his own. He was the one who had fallen into the well he had seen in the depths of the eyes of the mythological creature with the pointed ears. He woke in a panic, sprawled on the floor, shivering and consumed by anger. The fury burned not only for failing to help his father, but for failing himself—for not doing anything.

CONFUSED, HE SITS on the edge of the bed. Though uncertain what exactly has happened, he is convinced it was his fault. He tries to get to his feet and walk, but his knees shake and he collapses back onto the bed. After a short rest, he makes another attempt. This time he manages to stand up straight, but walking is difficult, his legs heavy as stone. Feeling trapped, he is spurred to try again. He perseveres, lifting each leg slowly, advancing from one end of the room to the other. After pacing back and forth a few times, he feels a slight sense of relief. He goes to the bookshelf and pulls down the chessboard his father gave him as a child.

He puts the board on the desk and arranges the worn, wooden pieces. First the red ones, then the yellow. He studies the setup, resisting the urge to move any of the pieces, unwilling to disrupt the symmetry of the two opposing sides. In his head, he plots strategies, imagining intricate scenarios. Then, with an unexpected burst of decisiveness, he reverses the order of things and opens with the red pawn to g5, immediately breaking the symmetry and responding from the other side with the yellow pawn to e4. He then brings out the red and yellow knights to conquer the center of the board. His moves are measured yet decisive. He jumps from side to side. The game forces him to simultaneously calculate contradictory moves, as if two different people lived inside him, hiding secrets from each other to sabotage the other's plans. His vision blurs, he pauses and holds his head between his hands. A throbbing headache crushes his skull, and he is no longer sure which of the two players is really him. After a few more moves, he raises his hand and, with a sweeping motion, knocks all the pieces over. He leans over the board, inspecting the pieces, strewn bodies across an abandoned battlefield. Then he straightens up, takes another swig from the whiskey bottle, rises slowly from his chair, goes over to the closet. He gets dressed, then returns to the desk.

He glances at the chessboard, gathers up the pieces from the table and floor, returns them to the box, folds the board, and leaves the room.

In the middle of the night, he wanders alone around the base. With unhurried steps, he crushes the gravel under his steel soles, and it seems to him that the crunching of the gravel merges with his heartbeats, creating a harmonious rhythm that defines his movement through both space and time, giving his life broader meaning.

When he reaches the chimp laboratory, he stops and lingers by the entrance. He slowly pulls a corrugated key out of his pocket, inserts it into the lock, and turns it with a soft click. He walks along the dark hallway toward the steel door leading to the ape enclosures. The enclosures are dim. He squints, straining to adjust his eyes to the darkness, attempting to distinguish between the murky shadows and the golden straw mattresses on which the chimpanzees lie. The intense concentration causes a sharp pressure between his temples. He holds his head in his hands, but the sensation intensifies, slicing like a scalpel through the lobes of his brain.

He leans against the wall, feeling his way along the hallway until he finds the light switch. He presses his thumb firmly on the switch. A faint hum resonates as the gas inside the neon tubes heats up. After a few flickers, the lights blink on, bathing the room in a sickly, greenish glow.

The chimps wake up, their eyes bleary. Through the steel bars, they appear innocent and lost. It is now clear to him

that neither he nor anyone else would ever be able to understand them. This thought fills him with a sense of purpose,
as if he has been imbued with a higher inspiration, the kind
that visits people in moments when they cannot perform the
role expected of them. With a few quick steps, he approaches
Ham's cage and opens the door. He moves to Enos's cage and
does the same. He continues cage after cage, setting each
chimpanzee free. At first, the apes hesitate to respond to his
invitation. After opening all the cages, Bradley steps back
and sits down on the floor in the center of the room.

Habakkuk is the first to venture out of his cage, followed
by Samuel, Elijah, and Johnny Weissmuller, named after the
legendary swimmer, who gained fame for his starring role
as Tarzan, the boy raised by apes in the African jungle. Next
come Elisha and Ham, Elkanah and Zechariah, and the rest of
the chimps. Initially, they converge and disperse throughout
the laboratory like a murmuration of starlings. They move
toward the kitchen, wandering around, climbing on chairs
and tables, overturning brimming ashtrays, opening closets,
and, ultimately, wreaking havoc on everything within their
reach. Though it appears they are sowing destruction, in
reality they are breathing new life into their surroundings.
Deborah, a chimpanzee with reclusive tendencies, separates
from the others and approaches the spirometer, the instru-
ment she is connected to every morning during respiratory
exercises and lung capacity tests.

She climbs onto the cold metal seat and detaches the gas
mask from the bracket, the same mask the technicians had
forcibly strapped to her head. She rips out the oxygen tube
and hurls it to the floor. Smacking her lips, she purses her
mouth, calling her friends to join her.

Johnny Weissmuller stands tall, gazing at his reflection in the large mirror affixed to the kitchen door. He lingers there, transfixed by the sight of the unfamiliar chimp. He approaches, extends a finger, touches the smooth glass surface and instantly recoils, pulling his hand back, retreating. But then suddenly, with a swing of his arm, he picks up a rice pot from the stove and flings it at the mirror. The glass shatters with a terrifying crash. Sharp shards fly through the air, bouncing on the floor, scattering in every direction, dispersing a fragmented mosaic of reflections into the surrounding space. The sound reverberates, the glass shards like clappers in a crystal bell, ringing inside the echo chamber of Bradley's head. In his imagination he sees a flame-engulfed forest.

One shard strikes Bradley's arm, slicing through the skin, cutting into the flesh. Another shard, shaped like an equilateral triangle, lodges perpendicularly in Enos's shoulder. A moan of pain escapes the chimpanzee's mouth, his face contorting into a grimace. Samuel notices Enos's distress and comes to his aid. Enos pounds the floor with his fist, while Samuel places one hand on his shoulder and grasps the base of the glass triangle with his other hand, attempting to extract it from his companion's flesh. Ape and human blood streams onto the floor, intermingling. Droplets splatter through the air, staining the kitchen walls and stove a deep crimson.

Toilet paper rolls hurl in every direction, unraveling across the floor. The chimps smash glasses and plates, rip cabinet doors from hinges, and watch them crash to the floor with ear-splitting noise. They turn on faucets, flooding the floor with water, diluting the blood, drowning the laboratory equipment already buried under trash and scattered stacks of paper.

The deafening noise awakens the camp guards. They rush to the laboratory, but halt momentarily at the entrance, stunned by the scene. They are lunging at the chimps, grappling to restrain them. Bradley retreats to the side, watching from the shadows as a gladiator battle unfolds between the uniformed guards and the hairy creatures. One guard gets bitten on the shoulder, another on the hand, but eventually all the chimps are subdued. The victorious guards shove each ape back into a cage. Bradley watches the apes gradually calm, their ragged breaths slowing, their movements becoming subdued. Eventually they arrange their straw mattresses and hunch over, as if apologizing for daring to rebel. Once all the locks are secured, the guards order Bradley to leave. They turn off the lights and exit the room. The chimpanzees, defeated and weary, nestle among the layers of straw and drift into sleep.

*　　*　　*

THE NEXT DAY, BRADLEY WAS SUMMONED TO A DISCIPLINARY meeting in the office of Hamilton Garbinsky, commander of the Department for Biological Experiments. Garbinsky informed Bradley in a low voice that he was dismissed, effective immediately.

Bradley stared at him with cold eyes, his face frozen, devoid of remorse. He did not reply to Garbinsky's words but felt a storm raging within him. It seemed that he and Garbinsky existed in parallel worlds, two straight lines sharing the same trajectory, with no chance of ever meeting.

Perhaps it was more accurate to think of them as two entities gazing at each other through concave lenses from opposite sides of a telescope. One brings you closer; the other draws you apart. Bradley shifted uneasily in his chair. "But what will you do with him afterwards?" he asked, "When he's no longer needed?"

Garbinsky shot him a look of disdain. "I think this conversation is over!" Bradley rose and left the room.

That evening, while cleaning the room after packing his belongings into his bag, he felt deep sorrow. The weight of his actions started to dawn on him. The moment of banishment had arrived, placing him at the edge of the abyss of loneliness that had always beckoned. He knew that he would never see Ham again. He approached the window and gazed through the pane at a thick-trunked sycamore tree. The gentle breath of the desert wind stirred the tree's wide canopy. He raised his eyes toward the silent face of the sky and stared for a long time at the few solitary stars that were visible through the clouds.

THE COLD, CLEAR LIGHT OF A SPRING MORNING heralds a new day, stirring the zoo to life. Ham opens his eyes. He gazes at a plastic space rocket painted the colors of the US flag. Fifty white stars arranged on a blue rectangle, and a red tip towers above them. This peculiar oversized toy is set in the center of the cage, like an unsightly growth. Outside, blue-breasted jays hop restlessly up and down the branches of a Douglas fir, searching for food. Among the green needles, a pair of gray squirrels playfully chase each other. The squirrels flick their tails as they climb nimbly up the trunk, blending into the bark and blurring until they disappear somewhere in the treetop.

Workers crouch on their knees, engrossed in weeding the flowerbeds, enriching the soil with potassium and nitrogen. The flowers are arranged in rigid geometric shapes, adorning the concrete expanses and steel bars with their vivid colors.

Swallows flit between the cages, gathering twigs, busy building mud nests in one of the food storage facilities at the far end of the zoo. They have recently returned, after an exhausting journey spanning oceans and deserts. Thousands of birds perished along the way from dehydration or starvation.

Every morning, visitors gather around the cage, curious to see the famous chimp, dwarfed by a plastic missile prop. Through the bars, the crowd strip away his skin with their eyes, licking his exposed flesh with their gaze.

Ham stares back at them. He watches them jostling and pushing. He has no comprehension of, nor would he ever comprehend, the urge that drives them.

They photograph him relentlessly, siphoning his identity into their dark boxes. With each flash, Ham blurs, his form dissolving within the limited depth of field captured by the camera lenses. He sits there, apathetic, watching without interest the crowd that never ceases to squabble over a spot at the front. With time, he learns to ignore them.

That morning, he sits with his back to them, peeling bananas and munching them slowly, with infinite patience. A mischievous child pushes to the front of the crowd. He calls out to Ham, teasing him to turn around, but the chimpanzee ignores him. The child loses patience and throws a few peanuts at Ham, which bounce off his back. A screech escapes Ham's throat, immediately met with cheers from the audience. People snicker and mimic his cry. The child, buoyed by the reaction, reaches into the bag of peanuts, grabs another handful and throws it. This time, Ham manages to dodge the barrage of peanuts, climbing to the top of the rocket and finding shelter in the cockpit.

He sits hunched over, folding his legs and arching his back over an imaginary seat. He closes his eyes and waits for a respite. He feels protected within the taut plastic walls. He lifts his head and looks through the bars at the sky, at the passing clouds.

He closes his eyes again, trying to fall asleep, perhaps in

an attempt to make time pass more quickly. Eventually the spectators give up, lose interest, return their cameras to their shoulder bags, and drift away. By the end of the day, as darkness falls, they exit the gates of the zoo. Nothing remains of this event except shades of gray stains burned onto rolls of film, traces of passing light waves.

HAM WAS NOT the first ape to become a symbol.

In 1630, the Dutch Prince of Orange received a gift: a young bonobo captured in what was then the Portuguese colony of Angola. He held her captive in the palace's private zoo. Until that time, no one in Europe had known of the existence of humanoids, and the young bonobo aroused a great deal of interest among the nobility. Dr. Tulp, a famous surgeon from Delft, sat by her side for days, observing and drawing her. He was convinced that she was a primal human. No one back then could have imagined that three hundred and thirty years later, a similar species of ape would be sent in a ballistic rocket toward the stars.

One hundred years later, in 1738, when zoos gradually began opening their gates to the general public, London introduced its first chimpanzee to curious spectators. The young madam, as she was called in the British press, was dressed in a silk smock and held in a cage designed as a doll's room. In the center of the cage stood a table surrounded by four mahogany chairs. Every weekend at five o'clock, in front of an enthusiastic crowd, she was served tea and biscuits. Despite being only two years old, she behaved like a lady in every way, and the newspapers marveled at her modesty, sweetness, and ability to walk on two legs and imitate human behavior.

One hundred and fifty years later, in a similar manner, a young Pygmy man named Ota Benga from the Mbuti tribe of the Ituri forests in the Congo Free State, then under Belgian colonial control, was exhibited in a monkey cage. Ota Benga, the man imprisoned in a zoo, became a sensation. Ota Benga had been captured by soldiers in the service of Belgian King Leopold II, after they murdered his wife and two children and burned down their village near the banks of the Kasai River. An American businessman named Samuel Philip Verner purchased him from a local slave trader, brought him to the United States, and loaned him to the Bronx Zoo. Hundreds of thousands of people flocked to see him in a cage he shared with an orangutan named Dohong. A traditional Mbuti hammock was installed in the cage, and Ota Benga was given a bow and arrow.

The act aroused the fury of African American religious leaders who demanded that he be treated not as a spectacle but as a human being. An article in *The New York Times* dismissed these claims, stating that Pygmies were at the bottom of the human ladder, and that freeing Ota Benga, treating him humanely, or educating him was absurd—a pointless waste of time and money.

Benga was burning up inside, lonely, and miserable. He refused to eat and sat in silence for hours in a corner of the cage, listening to the hollow sound of the steel bars, the murmur of derisive conversations, the click of heels on the concrete floor, and the helpless cries of wild animals trapped in nearby cages. He was like a tree that had been felled. His heart was filled with longing for his family, his friends, the sound of birdsong, for the rustle of leaves, the whisper of a passing breeze through the bushes. Sometimes he was gripped by fits of rage and threw objects at visitors. One day, he attacked a visitor and tried to stab him with a knife. Another day, he shot arrows at the crowd and almost hit a group of children. His behavior became unpredictable, and after a tortuous year, he was released from the zoo. Benga was sent to an orphanage and later adopted by a foster family in Virginia. He was educated by a local poet and worked in a tobacco factory. Yearning for his family and homeland stifled him, and his ties to reality gradually loosened. He withered like a flower wrenched from its stem. Then, one bleak March morning in 1916, he went alone to a clearing in the forest, gathered dry twigs, and built a traditional Mbuti bonfire, as he had been taught by the elders of his tribe. He removed his clothing and shot a hole through his heart with a stolen gun. His body was discovered beside the embers, all alone. He was buried anonymously and unceremoniously in an unmarked grave plot on the outskirts of a cemetery in Virginia.

*　　*　　*

SINCE LEAVING HOLLOMAN, BRADLEY WAS CONSUMED BY anguish. His act of revenge had filled him with a kind of childish pride but also plagued him like a relentless disease. Again and again, he turned over events of that night in his mind. Disturbing thoughts raced through his head like a herd of wild horses—the laboratory, the psychomotor devices, the sighs of despair, the flashes of longing for the scent of Ham's fur, and the resonance of his damp breath. He felt guilty, knowing his actions had left them both broken, somehow damaged, in spite of or perhaps because of their rigorous, scientific training and discipline. Anger coursed through him, an unyielding force. He wanted to do something meaningful. To atone for his sins. To spare Ham the injustices of the world. But fear paralyzed him. He convinced himself that, in the end, he would not be able to change anything. Since returning to New York, he had spent much time alone in a half-empty room of his small apartment. He sat in a captain's chair, by the light of an office desk lamp that shone above a beeswax-treated walnut surface, and wrote his childhood memories.

This was the apartment where he had grown up, left to him by his mother after she moved to a nursing home in Brooklyn.

In his youth, he had loved to wander the neighborhood streets, exploring the bustling stores, visiting the Natural History Museum, or riding his bicycle in Central Park. In those days, most of the residents of the Upper West Side were still Jews who had immigrated from Eastern Europe, but over the years, Black Americans from the South, Dominicans, Puerto Ricans, Russians, Ukrainians, and Cubans had moved in, making the area diverse and colorful.

He found a part-time job at the Botanical Garden in the Bronx, working only mornings and making sure to finish his shift before most visitors had arrived. In the spring, he fertilized the soil and weeded the rose garden. In the summer, he worked to the soothing sounds of a rustling stream in the wooded part of the Garden, where saplings were planted in memory of the trees that once blanketed the city before the arrival of European settlers. He watched robins splashing in water fountains, walked among beech and birch trees, and in the fall, after the flowers wilted, he trimmed their stems in preparation for winter dormancy.

He suffered from restlessness around other people, feeling as though a glass partition separated him from the rest of his species. He was certain that everyone was looking and pointing at him. No one, he was sure, understood his pain.

One day he received a letter from Diana Bayer, who wrote that she was moving to Pennsylvania. She had taken a new position at the university library, organizing the private archive of the late Donald Sandler, a zoologist and ornithologist. She explained that he had left behind manuscripts and a collection of rare books. She asked how Bradley was doing, whether he had been able to see Ham, and whether he would like her to stop by on her way to Pennsylvania. Bradley was fond of Diana, but he did not answer her letter. Diana's attempt to get closer caused him to withdraw. It made him feel hollow and helpless.

He found refuge in books, a vicarious escape into other people's lives. At every opportunity, he buried himself in pages chock-full of history, passion, and knowledge.

On the days when he was not working, Bradley visited the New York Public Library in the city center, whose front steps were flanked by a pair of white marble lions, Patience and Fortitude. He climbed one of the two wide staircases to the second floor. He walked by tall Corinthian columns, treading across variegated marble slabs along sun-drenched corridors. Dust particles trapped in sunbeams floating in the air appeared to him as arrows shot by angels through the ornate windows. On his way to his regular spot, he passed drowsy librarians seated behind long, smoothly polished service desks. Once he got to his habitual corner, he removed his coat and draped it over the back of a chair, at a table topped with green leather, embellished with gold stripes. The study tables were surrounded by shelves laden with books arranged like mummified bodies in an enormous catacomb. Hundreds of thousands of worn spines compressed into dense rows and columns. Each book was engraved with a name. Despite evidence of wear and tear, it seemed to him that time itself was suspended here. Past, present, and future mingled on the shelves. He closed his eyes and imagined how, through this heavenly silence, the ruins of the past returned to life. He saw the books as proof that the past was never lost, that there was always a chance to get back and repair what had been done. The thought consoled him. He felt secure in this alternative reality. It enveloped and protected him, operating according to a clear logical set of rules where every word had a reason and every sentence was justified. It comforted him to know that every detail had a place and no written sentence disappeared. He took off his shoes, polished the lenses of his glasses, and opened a book. His nostrils filled with the scent of aging paper. He lowered his head, turned the pages, settled down, and surrendered to the written words. His muscles relaxed, as if his body was weightless, and the words lifted him up, carrying him through boundless space, enabling him to float between continents. One moment he was in America, the next in Africa. He wandered through rainforests, learned about the beliefs of the Obi tribe on the Ivory Coast, who contended that chimpanzees were their free brothers who had been punished with ugliness when they had refused the divine command for all humans to carry out work. He discovered that the Mende tribe living in the forests of Guinea were also convinced that chimpanzees were descendants of a sacred nomadic tribe, and that the Baka tribespeople had a custom of burying chimpanzees alongside humans.

From there he continued to Siberia, where he learned about the ancient customs of the Katch people, who regarded forest bears as their wild and furry kin. Young couples who were unable to have children kidnapped bear cubs and raised them as their own. They pierced their ears and threaded hammered copper earrings into them. As the years passed and the bears grew up and lost their childish charm, they released them back into the forest. If by chance their paths crossed again, they immediately recognized each other, thanks to the copper earrings, avoiding an end that could have been fatal.

Bradley learned more about apes as well. He read about two chimpanzees, Mabel and Salome, who were raised in human families as daughters in every way. Both were ultimately abandoned and as a result became deeply depressed. They refused to eat or drink, and eventually died from severe bouts of diarrhea, diagnosed as dysentery. The same happened to Gua, the chimp who grew up as Donald's twin sister, the biological son of Winthrop and Luella Kellogg. Winthrop was a professor of behavioral psychology at Indiana University. He brought Gua to their home when she was eight months old to study the effects of their son Donald's development on her. But after a few months, when the couple noticed the experiment was having the reverse effect and young Donald was starting to behave like an ape, they grew concerned and eventually decided to part ways with Gua. She didn't understand what had happened and why she had suddenly been rejected, forced to live in a cage.

The dramatic change overwhelmed her: like Mabel and Salome, she didn't survive for long. A year later, she died of pneumonia.

Bradley thought about Enos, Ham's friend, who had died of dysentery four years after returning from his own space flight. After Enos's death, an autopsy was performed. According to the pathological report no causal link was found between Enos's death and the grueling training, headaches, electric shocks, gravitational pressure, cosmic radiation, heat, cold, deafening noise, floating in space, parachuting, ocean wave turbulence, and isolation.

*　*　*

ON THE EVENING OF JULY 20, 1969, AS NEIL ARMSTRONG planted the U.S. flag on the surface of the moon, Ham was alone. It had been a dizzying summer, as the United States swung between love and war, between hope and tragedy. The Vietnam War claimed many victims, and millions of people took to the streets to protest the pro-war administration. In upstate New York, two young men organized a music festival, and hundreds of thousands of flower children gathered at Woodstock, dancing and singing in the name of peace. Protest organizations united for social justice and equal rights for ethnic minorities, women and gays.

No one spared a thought for Ham.

The plastic rocket that decorated the cage gradually faded. The colors of the flag succumbed to the ravages of time, the heat of the scorching sun during the summer months, the dry cold of the dark winters, and the putrid humidity of the fall rains. Viscous, acidic bird droppings gnawed at the hard layers of paint, peeling off the protective skin, rendering the rocket worn and graceless.

The rocket, no longer of interest, was removed from the cage, dismantled, and thrown into a junkyard.

Ham had been sentenced to years of loneliness in the Washington Zoo. He was abandoned like an expired specimen rotting away among the weeds that grew through the gaps between the concrete cracks and the steel bars of the cage.

*   *   *

Winter. A generous moon illuminates the night sky. Soft snowflakes fall slowly, like angels exhaling their last breath. The flakes surrender to the forces of gravity, gently melting on the asphalt. A hush envelops the zoo. Ham is alone, watching this spectacle of heavenly beauty. The cold makes the follicles of his fur stand on end. Shivers wrack his body, causing his muscles to tremble. He hugs his body with his arms, digging his hands into his armpits. The zoo is empty of visitors. Through the bars, he watches a lamp as it turns on and off to the rhythm of a heartbeat. The lamps are spaced at regular intervals. A sequence of white points of light marks the paths through the zoo.

In the distance, he spies a guard walking up a narrow slope toward him. Ham follows the guard's clumsy movements. He hears the crunch of the soles of his boots as they etch tracks in the virgin snow. Crunch, crunch, his boots crush the snowflakes, forcing the soft powder to yield, compressing into a dense layer of treacherous ice against the frozen ground. Moving at a steady rhythm, the guard appears and then immediately disappears, reappears under a lamp, and is swallowed up again by the darkness. Gradually drawing near, the guard's figure grows larger with each step. He finally stops for a moment in front of the cage, gives Ham a tired look, takes a deep breath, exhales a jet of cold vapor toward him, turns around, and continues along his regular route. The guard walks away, receding with each step until he melts into the darkness.

Winters are hard on Ham. The emptiness of the garden, the unbearable cold. Every morning he watches crows hopping between dormant flower beds, rummaging with their thick beaks in the hard earth and snow, retrieving food stored back in the fall for times of need.

One morning, a little girl in a long red coat appeared by the cage with her mother. She stood there, quietly watching him. At first, Ham ignored the visitors. But when the girl stamped her foot, he turned around, faced her, and moved toward the front of the cage. When their eyes met, he stopped. They stood there, frozen, their eyes reflecting each other.

The girl's heart ached at the deep sadness exuding from him. She raised her hand in a failed attempt to wipe away a tear as it trickled down her cheek. He followed the tear, watching it freeze over as it descended, turning into an ice crystal.

The mother urged the girl to leave, but the girl ignored her, remaining frozen in her spot, gazing at Ham. The tears that filled her eyes rendered him blurry, his face dissolving into a mass of black fur. And as if in a dream, he began to change shape, turning into a liquid animal. She sensed him fading away. Abruptly, she turned and caught up with her mother. Ham was left alone in the garden of snow.

That night, Ham returned to the girl in a dream. He sat beside her on a gnarled tree trunk, one of several arranged in a circle. It was unclear whether the trunks had been arranged by human hands or whether nature had intended it so. The stars and moon hovered above their heads like the painting she had completed for a school competition when her class had learned about Apollo 11 landing on the moon. The Astronaut Waltz played in the background, the same music the teacher had played for them, with lyrics she knew by heart. They were alone in a strange landscape that resembled a stage set more than a natural environment.

Beyond the horizon, there was a muffled flapping of wings, followed immediately by the squeal of a desperate mole fighting for its life in the claws of a predatory night bird.

The girl's heart clenched like a fist. She clung to Ham and he wrapped his arms around her shoulders. Cautiously, she curved her body against his chest and surrendered to his simple embrace. She buried her face in his shaggy fur, but then awakened with a start, afraid that in another moment she might suffocate from the musty citrus smell emanating from him.

In the morning, she sat down and wrote a letter begging for Ham's release. She summed everything up in a short sentence: "He was so lonely, the sadness in his eyes made me cry." She gave the letter to her mother and asked her to send it to the newspaper.

The letter reached *The Washington Post's* editorial office. It touched the heart of a section editor, who published it and even sent a reporter to interview the zoo director.

*   *   *

ONE DAY, FOLLOWING THE ZOO DIRECTOR'S INSTRUCTIONS, the keepers attempted to move Ham from his solitary cage to a large enclosure where a family of chimps lived. Sensing their intention to move him, Ham became distressed and tried to resist. He climbed to the top of the cage, hooted loudly, and clung desperately to the cold metal bars. Eventually, the zookeepers sedated him. When he regained consciousness, he found himself in a large enclosure, behind a shut door. Ham woke up dazed and frightened, not daring to move.

Three males got up and lumbered over to him. Their body language was fierce; they had not come to inquire about his health. They screeched at him and shoved him into a corner. He tried to escape but there was nowhere to go. They pounced on him, they punched him, they bit him all over his body and spat on him. He cried out but none of the keepers dared to enter the cage. Finally, one of them ran to get a rifle and eventually fired a tranquilizer dart at Ham's attackers. The dart hit one of the males in the back and he immediately let go of Ham as he struggled to remove the dart lodged in his shoulder. The other two male chimpanzees panicked and retreated. Immediately after, the injured male collapsed with a dull thud onto the floor. He lay there as if dead, while Ham, sprawled on his back next to him, did not dare to move. Only after realizing his attackers had gone did he slowly get up and drag himself, bleeding and limping, toward the door. The two zookeepers rushed toward him and quickly took him out of harm's way.

Later in the spring, they tried to pair Ham with Maggie, a young female chimp who had grown up with the family in the large enclosure but had been ostracized by the other females of the group after a fall out with Mika, the alpha female. The zookeepers moved her into Ham's cage, but he remained apathetic. His zest for life seemed drained by the hardships he had endured. For most of the day, the two chimps sat far apart like display dummies in a wax museum. Ham's body had become mere material bound in misery. He no longer knew who he was or what he was doing. For days, the zoo veterinarians observed the two chimps' behavior, trying to devise creative ways to encourage interaction and attempting to foster a bond between them. Nothing worked. Eventually they gave up. Maggie was sent to the Lincoln Park Zoo in Chicago, and Ham returned to his isolation.

Ham's life in the zoo was like floating in space. Here, as in space, time had no meaning. Nights and days lost their identity, merging into each other in continuous chaos. He passed his days fossilizing on a pile of dry straw, floating in the void. All his memories had been erased. He was an ape without a past.

If he moved from his perch, it was usually toward a worn, gray truck tire that dangled in the center of the cage. A thick rope was wrapped around the tire, which hung from the ceiling. When waves of rage flooded him, he charged at the hard rubber casting, striking the ring and crushing it with great force between his arms. He tried several times to break the rope, to rip the tire from the ceiling. But at the end of every struggle, when he either despaired, lost interest, or resigned himself to his fate, he straightened up, grasped the rope in his muscular hands, hoisted himself into the air, threaded his legs through the ring, and settled down on the tire. Occasionally, he swung his legs in the air, reached up with his hands, grasped the upper part of the rope, and rested his cheek on his raised shoulder. He sat immobile like this for long hours, daydreaming and staring at the floor. At times, for no apparent reason, he crawled out of his shell and moved his body back and forth, swinging and rocking the tire from side to side like a pendulum hanging by a spring, swinging in simple harmony. In the evenings, he sat in the corner of his cage plucking hairs from the thinning fur of his coat. Bald white patches emerged on his arms, above his elbows, between his shoulder blades. Sometimes he walked to the front of the cage, stood on his hind legs, grasped the bars, and swayed compulsively.

* * *

IN A DREAM, BRADLEY FINDS HIMSELF SITTING IN FRONT OF Ham's cage at the Ape Lab in Holloman. He leans forward, opens the cage door, crawls inside, and closes it behind him. He arranges a stack of hay on the floor, curls up, and goes to sleep.

He dreams that he wakes to a loud clapping sound. When he opens his eyes, he sees two muscular security guards standing in front of the cage. They grab him and forcefully pull him out. They lead him along a gray-and-red checkered linoleum-covered hallway, heavy with the pungent scent of cleaning fluids. Bradley becomes lightheaded, feeling as though he is being sucked backward. He quickens his pace, trying to break free from their grip, but they are too strong.

When he finally wakes, he can hardly remember the dream—but Ham's image refuses to leave his mind. The more he tries to forget, the more vividly it lingers. He walks to the bathroom to wash his face. He turns on the tap and straightens up. Confused, he looks at himself in the mirror. And then—precisely then, in the midst of his confusion—a sudden urge rises within him: he must go to Washington and see Ham.

*   *   *

ON HIS WAY TO THE WASHINGTON ZOO, BRADLEY WALKS up Constitution Avenue. He strolls along under a vibrant sea of cherry blossoms. He stops and sits on a bench in the avenue, observing the pink flowers weaving into the blue sky like heavenly filigree. He follows the progression of the clouds, watching as they move between the branches. As he watches, the clouds grow thicker, drawing water vapor from the damp surfaces of the dehydrating green leaves.

In 1912, the Japanese gave the cherry trees, under which he now sits, as a gesture of friendship to the city of Washington. But during World War II, when relations turned hostile, local patriots cut down several trees on Constitution Avenue as an act of revenge. At the same time, Japanese kamikaze pilots took flowering cherry branches with them on suicide missions. In Japan, the pink flowers symbolize the fleeting beauty of life. The kamikaze pilots identified with the falling cherry blossoms, plunging to their deaths at the height of their glory, scorning Korean and Chinese flowers, which wilted on their stems and ended their lives in graceless misery.

Bradley sits on the bench in the avenue. The zoo opens in about an hour. His legs are slightly apart, his head bowed. He looks down at the ground, counting the faded petals that have fallen. As he counts, more and more petals fall.

A deluge of pink, covering the avenue's paths with a thick weave of flowers. He observes the sweet colors, the disintegrating petals swept along by the wind, landing on sidewalks and roads in their journey back to the earth.

He is the first visitor to arrive at the zoo.

Standing at the gates, cordoned off by steel and concrete, he notices a bronze statue of a lion, unwittingly crowned the king of all beasts. Now the lion sprawls alone on a grassy patch of green like a giant toy, polished to perfection in the image of a deity.

He buys a ticket and enters the zoo.

He walks along the winding path, bordered by vibrant ornamental gardens that remind him of Jan Brueghel's blooming flower portraits, which he encountered in his youth while visiting the Metropolitan Museum in New York with his mother. In the early seventeenth century, when European sailors returned from imperial voyages laden with unimagined treasures, Brueghel painted, with intense realism, perpetual blossoms from whose depths death cried out. In his paintings, exotic specimens collected from far-flung lands bloomed from ornate porcelain vases. The vessels were actually cages, asserting control over their captive splendor. The zoo is also a kind of vase, a network of cages populated by animals from different geographical environments, from all continents of the world: Australia, Africa, Asia, Europe, South and North America, Antarctica, and the Arctic. Large and small animals, furry and bald, in all shapes and colors of the rainbow. A spectacular display of depleted nature. Each cage is a frame, like a picture on a museum wall. He walks through the winding, orderly hallways of a rectangular building where rows of large, glass containers house boa constrictors, tropical river fish, poisonous frogs, invertebrates, and collections of arthropods. Adjacent to the rectangular building stands a round dome that shelters nocturnal creatures: vampire bats, jerboas, hedgehogs, and a pair of shy fennec foxes entrapped in artificial darkness, observing visitors through reinforced glass partitions.

He passes by the lion enclosure and notices how close it is to an enclosure housing a herd of Thomson's gazelles. He is surprised that the zoo's architect did not think to put the predator at a distance from their prey. He assumes that it must be insufferable to live this way, predator next to prey, in a prison of nightmares and stymied cravings. He feels the distress of the anxious gazelles, and immediately afterward reminds himself that the lions have no easy lives either. He assumes they have lost their minds; how does one live facing an unattainable temptation, a sensuous stimulation that ceaselessly deprives them of rest. Perhaps this proximity was forced upon them not by chance, but out of a malicious urge, a powerful craving, or a calculated decision to keep the animals in a constant state of excitement, and provide visitors with pleasure and satisfaction?

He rejects this possibility, thinking that even the project managers must have understood the inevitability of habit's dulling force. Over time, the gazelles would adapt, their initial terror eroding into a hollow vigilance, a mechanical reflex without meaning. Likewise, the lions would lose hope, their primal hunger dulled into a numb, listless acceptance. As they surrender to the rules of this new existence, a process of polishing, abrasion, and erosion will occur in their minds. They will no longer dream at night, and the sights, smells, and sounds of the landscapes in which they grew up will fade from their memory. Finally, when no trace remains of their past, their desires will dissolve too, and then, by the grace of forgetfulness, perhaps their suffering will cease and they will live in peace in the new reality forced upon them.

Bradley arrives at the primates exhibit, greeted by a welcome sign adorned with the stylized silhouette of an upright chimpanzee. Beyond the sign is a tall, arched enclosure housing a family of Angolan colobus primates. He marvels at the sight of their black fur with contrasting white stripes that frame their shoulders and faces. The exuberant monkeys are enjoying themselves, playing on the climbing apparatus built for them. They climb and jump between severed branches of dry, leafless trees. For a long while, he watches a female colobus who sits alone on a branch in a corner of the enclosure. She is nursing an infant, her face serious. It moves him to think that, despite everything, she is still driven by the need to devote herself to her baby and escape the artificial world in which she is imprisoned.

He turns right, passing cages of spider monkeys, crested gibbons, and gray langurs. From afar, he spies the hominid enclosures—orangutans and chimpanzees.

He approaches cautiously.

Among the enclosures, he notices an isolated cage housing a large, muscular chimpanzee. Bradley recognizes him right away. He watches him through the camouflage fencing, an obstruction he perceives as the final lock on the world. He struggles to restrain a burning urge to go up to the cage and break it, to open a window and bring Ham back into the free world, airy and boundless.

He lowers himself cautiously onto a bench, intently

examining the movement of Ham's body from afar. He notes the matted fur and watches the chimp as he bends over the trough, drinking blackened water. When Ham has drunk his fill, he lifts his head from the trough and opens his mouth wide in an agonized yawn. Then he straightens up, stands on his hind legs and clumsily drags himself from the trough toward a rope ladder hanging from the ceiling. He sits under the ladder on the concrete floor, his back to the crowd. By his side is a pile of apples given to him by the zookeepers on the breakfast round. He extends a long arm toward the apples, grabs one of them and examines its peel with his fingers. Then he places the apple back on the floor, and extends his arm again, scooping up a few scattered apples and rolling them back to the pile. He picks up another apple and puts it in his mouth.

Bradley remains seated, patiently following Ham's actions.

Overhead the azure of the sky is gradually fades as burning yellow and orange hues begin to fill the horizon.

As if woken from a dream, Bradley glances at his watch. To his surprise, it is quite late in the afternoon.

He rises from the bench and approaches Ham's enclosure without taking his eyes off the solitary ape pacing back and forth as the setting sun casts its light on the cage.

He closes his eyes and then opens them again, fixing his gaze on Ham's thick fur, as if hoping its blackness will shield him from the fluttering moths he feels in his head, gnawing his brain, crumbling him from within. Then, without warning, their gazes meet. It is like a flash of lightning that precedes a deafening rumble of thunder. The meeting of their eyes ignites the space between them with an electric charge, pulling them toward each other.

In that split second, Ham springs from where he was sitting and with a few mighty leaps advances to the front of the cage. He grabs the steel bars and rattles them, striking them with a tremendous force that makes the metal tubing vibrate, a resounding clang of cold cymbal clashes. He opens his mouth wide, baring formidable fangs that have grown and sharpened over the years. Then, like a knife plunged into a heart, a deep screech of despair bursts out of him, emptying his lungs and turning into a prolonged howl until he chokes, his voice cut off with a strangled gasp. The noise arouses the curiosity of other visitors, and some of them hurry to witness the event. Their presence intensifies Ham's distress, and he begins to beat himself again, throwing his body against the cage bars compulsively.

Without warning, in the heat of the moment, he bends down, snatches a red apple from the pile gathered beside the trough of blackened water, and hurls it forcefully through the cage bars toward the crowd. Ham repeats the action, again and again. Blow after blow, he pelts the crowd with rotten apples that strike, bruise, drip, and smear across the faces of the visitors.

The surprise attack creates pandemonium. Children are hit, mothers shield toddlers with their own bodies, fathers spread arms and legs to protect loved ones. The crowd scrambles to get away from the cage, calling for help. Amidst the cacophony, Bradley stands immobile, frozen. He remains silent. The two of them are very close to each other, trapped in a moment that defines their essence. It reminds Bradley of a scene in a movie where a man is standing and gazing at his own reflection in a worn bathroom mirror. In the film, the man holds a gun in his hand, aims at his reflection, and challenges himself, mumbling as he squeezes the trigger, "Here is a man who would not take it anymore." Here is a man no longer willing to bear the injustices of the world, a man who has come to lift the shroud of suffering. As Bradley stands and observes, he feels the taut muscle fibers, his fingers tensing as if drawing an arrow across a bow.

Suddenly, a shot rings out. He sees the chimp tossed into the air, turning from side to side, falling heavily and crashing to the ground. Bradley's entire body shudders. A deathly silence descends.

Bradley turns his head and sees guards in blue uniforms. Holding rifles, they run toward the cage, ordering the crowd to disperse. Through glazed eyes, he detects two people dressed in white coats. They have entered the cage and lean over Ham, who lies unconscious, sprawled on the ground, his arms outstretched, his face glistening with apple pulp.

*   *   *

WHEN HAM WAKES UP, HE FINDS HIMSELF IN A STICKY puddle, soaked in urine, confined in a unfamiliar cage reinforced with wire mesh. An isolated cage devoid of history, defining for him the territory of no choice. To a free being, all cages may appear the same, but to the apes imprisoned within them, each cage holds its own distinct despair.

He scratches his fur obsessively, as if trying to dig deep enough to reach the sorrow buried inside him. He rubs his rear end against the cold floor, rises unsteadily, whimpers weakly, and lets himself collapse back to the ground. Curled up like a fetus, he lies motionless.

The night is cold beneath a cloudless sky. He pulls his

knees to his chest, wrapping his arms tightly around them as a spasm of chills passes through his body.

His cage, at the North Carolina Zoo, is located on the outskirts of the compound, far away from the crowds, serving as a temporary dwelling. Soon they will transfer Ham to his new home at an ape rehabilitation center, known as the Lonely Hearts Club.

The rehabilitation center is a larger enclosure with hundreds of square feet of green grass, a steep slope, palm trees, climbing frames, and hammocks. An artificial paradise designed to provide chimpanzees with peace and contentment.

A small family of five chimps lives in this compound, one male and four females. Maggie and Tamai were both born in the zoo and transferred to the rehabilitation center because of their mild temper. Having grown up among their own kind, they are skilled in social etiquette, helping traumatized chimps adjust to their new environment. The other three chimps each carry a difficult past, their own tragedies etched into their beings. Some were born in rainforests, others in research laboratories or circuses. Without exception, they have been abducted and orphaned.

Hemingway, the dominant male and leader of the group, arrived at the compound from Dr. Sam Ridley's research institute. Ridley was known for treating his chimpanzees severely. He regarded himself as their king and would randomly give them electric shocks with a prod, humiliating them in front of the others to assert his superiority. He claimed to have learned this in the circus, insisting that only through force could wild animals understand who their leader was. Hemingway, who became the alpha male of the institute, was nicknamed Satan by Ridley. Once, when Hemingway defiantly spat on him, or as Ridley claimed, "forgot his place," he went to his office, returned with an air rifle, and shot bursts of pellets at his legs until Hemingway collapsed on the cage floor, lying submissively on his back. Ridley then sedated him, pulled a sharpened butcher's knife from the backpack, and thrust the sharp blade into Hemingway's flesh, digging out the pellets from the ago-nized chimpanzee's shins and thighs. From that day on, every morning when he entered the laboratory, he forced Hemingway to get down on all fours, crawl toward him, bow his head, and kiss the silver ring he wore, adorned with a snake engraving and ruby stones.

Gradually the constantly humiliated Hemingway became unpredictable and would occasionally lash out at weaker chimps. One day, without any apparent provocation, he attacked a young male chimpanzee, bit him in the face, and fatally wounded him. When the victim was sprawled on his back, he spread his legs, sunk his teeth into his groin and tore off his testicles.

Another chimpanzee, Frida, is the matriarch of the family and Hemingway's preferred mate. She had been wrenched away from her mother when she was two days old. Frida was sold to a small circus called the Animal Box where they trained her with clubs and whips. They often punished her, confiscating her toy doll, kicking her when she refused to obey their commands, starving her and locking her for hours in a dark kennel. They usually fed her leftover food from garbage cans. Every evening, they led her to the center of the ring in the threadbare tent and forced her to dance and entertain the cheering audience. Frida was repeatedly punished with a whip till she learned to obey and perform on command. Her specialties included tightrope walking and acrobatics. She was also trained to play the trumpet and keep her balance while standing on the back of a galloping pony. Despite these difficult conditions, she grew. When she was six years old, she became so strong and stubborn that Marilyn Copperfield, her trainer, was unable to assert control over her. One day, when Copperfield whipped Frida because she refused to climb onto the pony's back, Frida shoved her against a wall and ripped a finger from her hand. After this incident, the circus owners gave Frida to the North Carolina Zoo, which was just starting out with its rehabilitation project.

Grace had arrived from a drug testing laboratory in Maryland. The laboratory technicians had been unaware that her mother was pregnant and were surprised to discover one morning that she was nursing a day-old infant.

When Grace was four months old, she experienced a violent seizure. The laboratory workers suspected epilepsy and, without thinking twice, performed surgery on her under full anesthesia. During surgery, they opened the baby chimpanzee's skull and separated her brain lobes. In effect, Grace had two disconnected lobes that didn't communicate with each other. The recovery did not go smoothly. Grace's head swelled due to internal bleeding, and the doctors had to perform additional surgery to drain the blood. During rehabilitation, she suffered from terrible headaches. A doctor named James Borman took pity on her and brought her home for the recovery period. Borman's wife and their three children cared for her devotedly until she regained strength, and she became part of their family. Since the laboratory had plenty of apes and monkeys, Dr. Borman managed to convince them to relinquish Grace.

For the first few years, everything went smoothly—Grace was tamed and integrated well into family life. But as she grew and reached sexual maturity, she became aggressive toward strangers.

One day, when Grace was five years old, she shattered the large living room window overlooking the garden, charged into the backyard, and attacked and tore to shreds the neighbors' German shepherd dog, Ernest, who had wandered into her territory. After this incident, the Bormans reluctantly decided that they must part with Grace and handed her over to the North Carolina Zoo.

*   *   *

HAM STANDS AT THE ENTRANCE TO THE ENCLOSURE, hesitating. The gate closes behind him. He presses his back against the barred fence, warily observing the group of chimpanzees gathered at the bottom of the slope. Maggie notices him first. Slowly, she climbs up the grassy slope toward him. When she is close to him, she extends her hand in a gesture of curiosity and reassurance, but he remains unresponsive. Hemingway has closely observed the interaction from a distance. Straightening up, he thumps his fists against his chest in a display of dominance. His fur bristles as he suddenly charges up the slope toward Maggie and Ham. On the way, he grabs an empty aluminum container and hurls it to the ground with an ear-splitting crash. Startled, Ham instinctively curls up, pressing himself flat against the floor. Just as Hemingway is about to lunge at him, Maggie steps forward, positioning herself between the two. The surprised Hemingway stops dead in his tracks. He glares at her, bares his fangs, but after a tense moment, lowers his head and retreats, deferring to Maggie's silent authority.

*   *   *

BRADLEY WAKES UP IN THE MIDDLE OF THE NIGHT drenched in sweat. The meeting with Ham at the Washington Zoo loops in his mind. He gets up, washes his face, smokes a couple of cigarettes. After sunrise, he drags himself to the kitchen and forces down a light breakfast—coffee and half a slice of toast. But the thoughts are insistent and unshakable. After placing the plate and cup in the sink, he picks up the phone and dials Oklahoma, the Institute for Primate Studies, located in the small town of Norman, near the university where he had once been a student.

The phone rings a few times. His heart pounds with each unanswered tone. Between rings, he feels a strange mix of anticipation and relief. His pulse races—one hundred and twenty or maybe even more. Just as he is about to give up and put the receiver back in its cradle, a man's voice answers. For a moment he hesitates, wondering if this is Kaine, but he quickly dismisses the idea and asks if Dr. Kaine is available.

"Who's calling?"

He replies that his name is Bradley, Bradley Rose. He explains that he's a university graduate, that he worked at the institute years ago as Dr. Kaine's assistant.

The man introduces himself as Bob Handley. He was an assistant for years, helping take care of Washoe, the famous chimpanzee of Roger Fouts and Allen and Beatrice Gardner, who was transferred from the University of Nevada.

Today, Bob says, he's an activist for chimpanzee rights. He mentions that the institute is in the process of shutting down, and that he's here to arrange the final transfer of the apes to a rescue center. He explains that Dr. Kaine no longer works at the institute and then asks how he can help.

Bradley falls silent, taken aback by Bob's response. He struggles to find the right words, his mind racing. Finally, he explains that he has a lone male chimp raised in Holloman, born in Cameroon, and that he is looking for a way to return him to Africa. Bob questions him further, asking how old the chimp is and where he is currently located. Bradley explains that the chimpanzee is now in a zoo, and that he was responsible for him while working at Holloman. "You've probably heard of him," he added, "he was the first chimpanzee NASA sent into space."

Bob pauses for a moment. "Do you mean Ham?"

Bradley nods silently, his grip tightening on the phone.

Bob asks, "Have you heard of a chimpanzee named Lucy?"

Bradley says no, and Bob continues, explaining that a book was recently published called *Lucy—Growing Up Human*, which tells her story. "She was born here at our institute and when she was a month old, Dr. Kaine separated her from her mother and handed her to Jane Temerlin, his secretary. The Temerlins raised her as if she were their daughter. I suggest you talk to them. For twelve years, she lived in their home. They treated her just like a human being.

"You see, the whole approach was fundamentally problematic. When I arrived here, I thought I'd reached paradise. I believed we were on the verge of a cognitive breakthrough, that together with the chimpanzees we were going to change the world. But over time, I realized how problematic every-thing we did here was. How can you really examine an ani-mal's behavior if you separate it from its own kind?

"The Temerlins were in denial. They taught Lucy table manners, to eat from china plates, and to dress herself in clothes made for her. She even slept with them in their double bed. But as Lucy grew older she became increasingly difficult to handle. Guests and neighbors stopped visiting, afraid of the ape. About three years ago, Jane found her mas-turbating with the vacuum cleaner in their bed and realized there was no choice; they had to let her go. They turned to Janis Carter, who worked here at the institute. Janis told them about Project Gambia, which prepared chimps raised in captivity to return to the wild. Jane and Morris Temerlin were excited by the idea and, together with Janis, organized a trip to Africa. Janis was supposed to stay with Lucy in the rehabilitation island for the first few weeks. But Lucy became depressed. She wouldn't leave Janis for a moment and insisted on drinking only from bottles. She refused to eat unless Janis peeled fruit and fed her from a plate, with a knife and fork. Janis couldn't abandon Lucy like this. It took almost a year before Janis managed to detach herself."

Bob falls silent. Bradley is not sure if he is still on the line. He strains to hear and catches the sound of deep, labored breaths. For a moment, it seems to Bradley as though he has vanished, replaced by an exhausted whale struggling to draw in oxygen to survive. After what feels like an eternity, Bob finally breaks the silence.

"This story doesn't have a happy ending," he says. "About six months ago, Janis went back to visit Lucy on Baboon Island—that's the name of the island where Lucy lived with her chimpanzee family—but she wasn't there. Janis searched for her everywhere until finally she found her—that is—her body. The poachers who had killed her had chopped off her hands and feet. Lucy had probably run toward them, eager as always to meet people. She was naive, and perhaps what happened was inevitable."

Unsure of what to say, Bradley mutters a quiet thank you and hangs up.

*   *   *

HE DOESN'T HEAR THE NEWS ON THE RADIO ABOUT HAM'S death. It is only the next day, at the library, that he reads about it in the newspaper. He sees Ham's picture on the third page of *The Washington Post*. The caption reads: "Ham, the first Astrochimp to fly to space in 1961 in a Mercury-Redstone rocket, died yesterday of heart failure, age twenty-six, in the North Carolina Zoo."

The obituary states that Ham was trained at Holloman Air Force Base after arriving there from the Cameroon rainforests when he was just a few months old. In the concluding paragraph, Peter Asker, spokesman for the Pathological Institute in Washington, mentions that Ham's body will undergo a four-week autopsy to study the effects of space travel and assess any potential damage. Bradley gasps. He feels lightheaded, as if all blood suddenly drained from his head to his feet.

He closes his eyes and breathes slowly, trying to steady himself. The shock lingers, then gradually dulls. After a while, as the noise in his head begins to fade, he stands up and walk out of the library and into the street, moving through the crowd. None of the dozen strangers inside had looked up—each lost in their own private world.

At home Bradley makes himself a cup of tea. He sits and watches the tea bag slowly stain the water in shades of brown and russet. He doesn't take his eyes off it until the water is fully infused. He removes the still-hot tea bag and tosses it in the trash, then sits quietly, waiting for the tea to cool. Steam spirals upward, dispersing into the air and fading into the room. Taking the cup, he goes to his small study, opens a drawer, and pulls out a faded cardboard envelope. Inside is the photograph Ralph Brady gave him a few days after they had dined together in Holloman, the one featured on the cover of *Life* magazine. It shows Ham, the young chimp in a spacesuit, lying on his back in a molded metal capsule. His arms are folded, his eyes closed. On his face is an angelic expression like that of a sleeping baby, or a prophet in a moment of revelation. The image holds Bradley's gaze.

He turns the photograph over and reads Ralph Brady's short dedication:

"To dear Bradley Rose, a moment that passed and became a memory, the beginning of a circle and also its end."

A Visit to Monkey World—
Ape Rescue Centre

DORSET'S MONKEY WORLD IS A ZOO, BUT NOT JUST any zoo. Dorset's Monkey World is a rehabilitation center for primates. All the apes here are survivors, chimpanzees who have undergone trauma, each one with his or her own sad story. In total, fifty-four chimpanzees live here, in four different areas, with every family having its own area. The smallest family is Bryan's, consisting of four chimps. Bryan, the head of the family, is a handsome, strong male, but because he grew up in deplorable conditions, he remains anxious and fearful. He suffers from anxiety attacks, and when they erupt, he hits himself hard, punching his own face and sometimes pulling out his hair and biting himself until he bleeds. Bryan was rescued from Mexico, where he was used as a prop by a wandering beach photographer. He has only four teeth left in his mouth; the photographer extracted all the others when Bryan was a year old to prevent him from biting children who came to have their photos taken with him. When Bryan arrived at Monkey World, he underwent a series of routine examinations, and they found a milk tooth secreted in his gums that had probably been stuck there for years. Initially, several attempts were made to integrate him into the family of an alpha male named Hananya. This family consists of ten apes, rescued from various places around the world, some from animal testing laboratories in France, some from circuses in Lebanon and Spain, and a chimp called Semach, rescued from a drug dealer in Israel. All these attempts failed, because Bryan lacked confidence and Hananya was wary of competing males. Every time Bryan was introduced into their enclosure, Hananya and Semach immediately attacked him.

Bryan's group includes three other apes besides himself—two females named Lulu and Naree, and a young male named Kangoo.

Lulu comes from a circus in Cyprus. She has only one arm; her mother bit the other arm when she was a baby, wounding her shoulder. The wound became infected, turned gangrenous, and the arm had to be amputated.

Naree comes from Thailand. Like Bryan, she has no teeth, but her condition is worse. Naree has a flattened nose and distorted face. Her caretakers believe the distortion was caused by a sinus infection, triggered by violent tooth extractions. As a result, the area became inflamed and the bone began to grow disproportionately. This distortion gives Naree a touching, human-like appearance. It's hard not to notice her. I sit and watch her for a long time, observing how Bryan and Kangoo, the young male who joined the group about a year ago, groom the hair on her back. She appears relaxed, sitting between them, and then suddenly turns to Bryan and pulls his eyebrows. It can't be particularly pleasant, but he doesn't object and allows her to do as she wishes.

Without teeth, she can't eat solid food, but Naree

manages quite well because her group members take care of her, chewing the tough fibers for her and offering her pre-chewed food.

The great love story in this small family is between Kangoo and Bryan.

Kangoo came to the rescue center from the Buenos Aires Zoo, where he grew up together with Sasha, his mother. Sasha is also his sister, because Sasha's father was her mate, and Kangoo's father is also his mother's father, so in a sense, he is also Kangoo's grandfather. I tried to find out the name of Kangoo's father-grandfather, but the keepers in the park could only say that after his death, Kangoo and Sasha were left alone, and since the Argentinian zoo authorities had decided to no longer keep foreign animals and focus only on local species, they found a new home for them.

The acclimatization of Sasha and Kangoo in Dorset's Monkey World was not easy. Prior to their arrival here, they had spent their lives in a small cage and had never met other chimps.

In a sense, Kangoo had been Sasha's chimpanzee all his life, and because she was very possessive, when they first arrived at Dorset, Sasha didn't allow him to go near any of the other chimps. Whenever he tried, she pulled him toward her and separated them. She was most wary of Bryan, and every time Kangoo and Bryan tried to communicate, Sasha intervened. After figuring out that physical proximity threatened Bryan, she made a point of standing close to him and staring hard, making him anxious and miserable.

This nightmare continued until the keepers discovered the problem and separated Sasha and Kangoo, moving Sasha from Bryan's small family to Hananya's. Since then, tensions have eased. Sasha has integrated well into her new family, while Kangoo and Bryan are now a couple.

In appearance, Bryan and Kangoo are very different from each other. Bryan is upright and muscular, while Kangoo is hunched over and gangly. Kangoo has a light, pinkish, hairless face and large Dumbo ears. His facial structure resembles a system of elliptical hoops seamlessly connected. The sunken cheekbones emphasize an expansive, rounded jaw, above which protrudes a small, inverted heart-shaped nose, grooved along its length by a vertical cut. The nose is wide and flat, as if the bridge of bone has been compressed and turned it into a smooth, almost homogeneous surface. The upper part of the face is delineated by a pair of concave arches framing the eye sockets, which shelter large dreamy amber eyes.

In contrast, Bryan has a tough, dark, and flattened face, full of wrinkles. The eyes, nose, and mouth are very close together, as if all the facial features are compressed into one mass, and this density gives Bryan's face an intense, wild, and tormented expression. Bryan's nose is large and well-defined, and by contrast his eyes are small and sunken. Bryan's ears are also small, but unlike Kangoo's, they are erect and proportional to the structure of his skull. Despite such striking physiological differences, the two apes are drawn to each other. Kangoo admires Bryan and follows him everywhere. The keeper reports that since they came to be together, Bryan is more relaxed and has almost stopped harming himself. It seems they complement each other; perhaps Kangoo has found a father figure in Bryan, while Bryan has found comforting companionship.

I sit and watch them. Kangoo gathers colorful remnants

of fabric and arranges them in a circle around himself. He repeats this action frequently, as if trying to build himself a nest for the night, but this time, as always, the attempt fails and he gives up, abandoning the fabrics and leaping toward Bryan. Bryan invites him to come closer, they link arms and embrace quietly.

Lulu and Naree rest on two synthetic tree trunks on the other side of the enclosure. Between the two trunks, red stretchy climbing ropes are suspended, and a worn rope ladder hangs from the top of the tree trunks.

Evening descends on the park. I glance at my watch; it's already five o'clock, and in a few minutes, they'll close the rescue center. The last visitors are making their way toward the exit.

Two keepers approach with a basket of fruit, enticing the apes to their sleeping quarters. All respond to their call except Lulu, who insists on staying outside.

I follow them, watching through the glass window. Bryan sits close to the window, a twist of orange peel protruding from his mouth. He stares into the distance, rolling half an orange between his lips. I press against the window and observe him closely; he continues as he was, ignoring me as if I'm not there. Now Lulu joins, too. The four of them sit, each both alone and together, devouring their dinner before nightfall.

I get up and leave. On my way out, I recall the keeper's words as he explained to two visitors that chimpanzees are social creatures and that the trauma of all these apes stems from being separated from their families and growing up alone. I think about Ham and the traumas he went through, snatched from his mother, the cruel training in Holloman

Air Force Base, enduring a harrowing spaceflight, and living life marked by perpetual pain and loneliness. Ham, I think to myself, is present in each of the chimpanzees living here, and to each of them I dedicate *Ham's Heaven*.

ORI GERSHT

London, England, 2025

AUTHOR'S NOTE

Ham's Heaven is a work of fiction based on historical events.

All the characters in the story are products of my imagination. Some are based on real individuals, but even in these cases, their names have been changed.

During the writing process, I examined many manuscripts and photographs, which formed the cornerstone of my research and on which I based my descriptions of Ham and his formative surroundings. I also drew on the stories of Washoe, Nim, and Lucy, chimpanzees raised in human environments who were part of experiments in which scientists examined the ability of chimpanzees to integrate into human society and use language similarly to humans. Especially useful were the following:

Nim Chimpsky: The Chimp Who Would Be Human, by Elizabeth Hess.

Next of Kin, by Roger Fouts.

Lucy: Growing Up Human: A Chimpanzee Daughter in a Psychotherapist's Family, by Maurice K. Temerlin.

APPENDIX: PHOTOGRAPHS

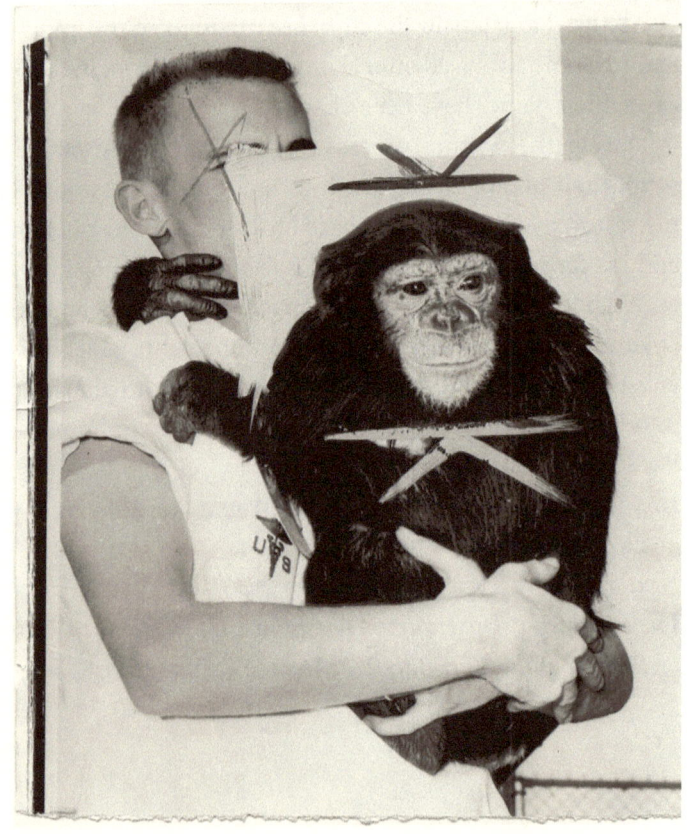

1. Ham in Bradley's arms, Holloman Air Force Base, Alamogordo, New Mexico, 1960. Photographer unknown.

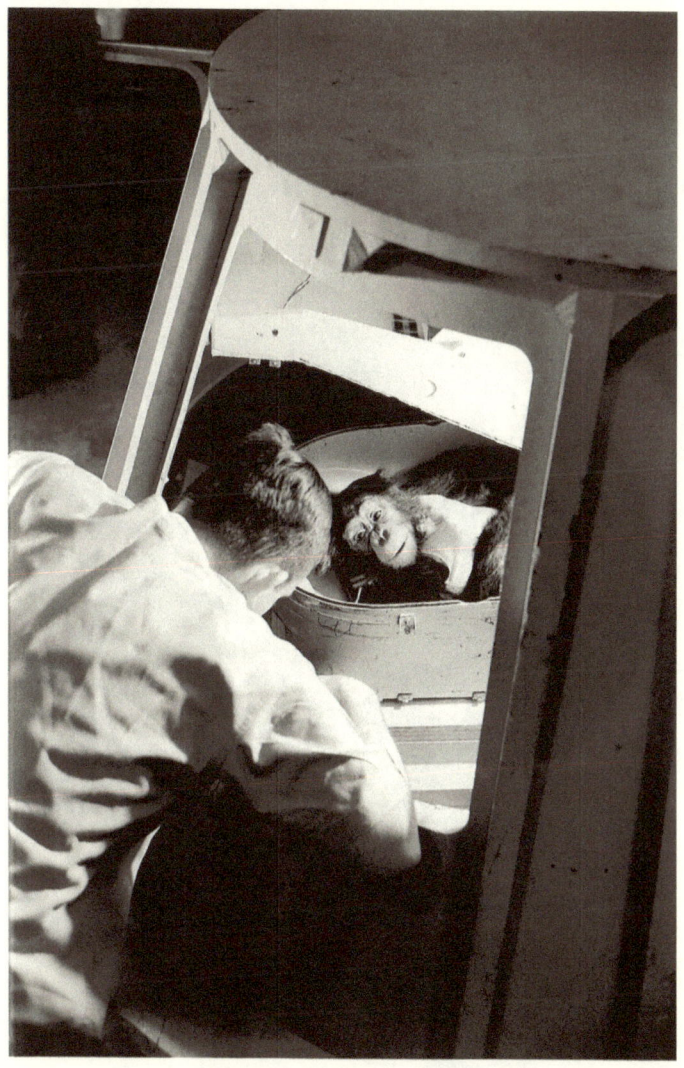

2.   Ham in flight training, vacuum chamber, Holloman Air Force Base, Alamogordo, New Mexico, 1960. Photographed by Ralph Morse, *Life* magazine (Shutterstock/Life Pictures/Ralph Morse).

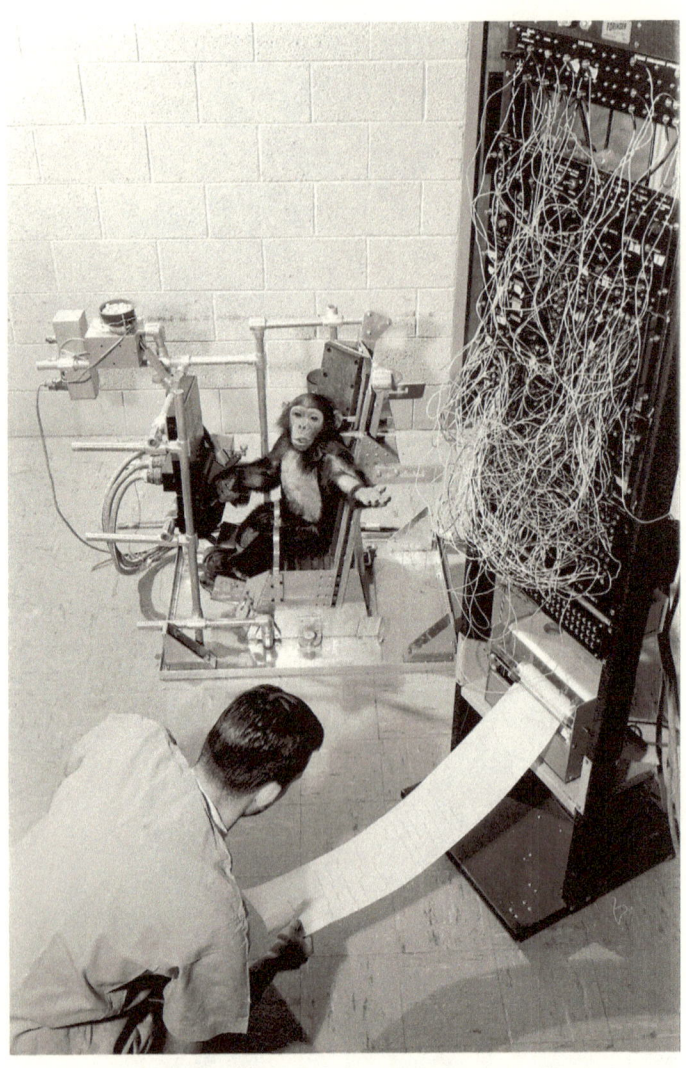

3. Ham and Bradley training on a psychomotor device, Holloman Air Force Base, Alamogordo, New Mexico, 1960. Photographed by Ralph Morse, *Life* magazine (Shutterstock/Life Pictures/Ralph Morse).

4.   Ham and Bradley walking toward the trailer, Missile Launch Base, Cape Canaveral, Florida, 1961. Photographed by Ralph Morse, *Life* magazine (Shutterstock/Life Pictures/Ralph Morse).

5.   Ham in space suit is fitted into the couch of the Mercury-Redstone capsule prior to its test flight on January 31, 1961. Courtesy NASA.

6. Ham holding Bradley's hand after returning from space, Missile Launch Base, Cape Canaveral, Florida, 1961. Photographer unknown.

ACKNOWLEDGEMENTS

Nogah Engler Gersht, my beloved wife—who accompanied me throughout Ham's journey, supported unconditionally, encouraged, and provided honest and uncompromising feedback. Also to our dear children, Amos and Lia.

Joanna Chen, for translating the book from Hebrew into English.

Mary Bahr of Warbler Press, for having faith in *Ham's Heaven*, for the undivided attention and commitment.

Ulrich Baer of Warbler Press, for having faith in *Ham's Heaven* and for the invaluable feedback in the editorial process.

The Israeli Institute for Hebrew Literature, for its support.

Ayelet Dan, for valuable editorial comments on the manuscript.

Yoav Rinon, for the support, and for the introduction to 9 Lives Press.

Uriel Kon and the entire 9 Lives Press team, for the trust they placed in me and in *Ham's Heaven*.

Amir Eshel, for support and for recommending the book to Warbler Press.

www.ingramcontent.com/pod-product-compliance
Lightning Source LLC
Chambersburg PA
CBHW052010240626
47153CB00008B/2811